Praise for
The Disassembled Man

"*The Disassembled Man* is lean and mean—with the emphasis on mean—a true psycho-noir novel that leaves the reader to work out the truth behind events we can only see from the point of view of the protagonist. *The Disassembled Man* is a damn fine read; a brilliant and raw example of the Psycho-Noir genre."

—Russel D. McLean, Crime Scene Scotland

"Jon Bassoff's *The Disassembled Man* is one strictly for the purists, the basement crazies, the inmates that are so fucked up that they don't even know they're in the asylum—much less able to run the fucking thing. This shit ain't for the casual crime fans. No, sir, dear readers, *The Disassembled Man* is for the folks who want their pulp served rare, as in still pumping steaming hot fucking blood. So yeah, you could say I dug the holy fuck out of it."

—Peter Dragovich, Book Central Station Review

"Bassoff has written sheer, nasty beautiful prose with this book. The wince factor is high and the characters horridly riveting. The envelope has not just been pushed, but set on fire."

—*Crimespree Magazine*

"Jim Thompson's psychotic hell brutally collides with Bruce Jay Friedman's absurdist humor in this shotgun blast of a novel."

—Dave Zeltserman, author of *Small Crimes*

THE DISASSEMBLED MAN

ALSO BY JON BASSOFF

Corrosion
The Incurables
Factory Town
The Blade This Time

JON BASSOFF

THE
DISASSEMBLED
MAN

Down & Out Books
3959 Van Dyke Rd, Ste. 265
Lutz, FL 33558
www.DownAndOutBooks.com

Cover design by Daniele Serra

ISBN: 1-946502-35-9
ISBN-13: 978-1-946502-35-3

For Allan Guthrie

CHAPTER 1

I was hunched over a trash can vomiting an evening's worth of burritos, whiskey, and misery, when this burly fellow reeking of sweat and two-dollar cologne grabbed me by the shoulders, spun me around, and slammed his meaty fist into my jaw. I performed a drunken pirouette, mumbled a pair of Hail Marys, and crashed to the alley asphalt. He stood over me and grinned. With pockmarked cheeks, a flattened nose, and a cruel mouth, he had a face that even a blind mother couldn't love. Not that I'm one to talk.

"Scarlett told me about you," he said. "She told me *all* about you."

"What the hell are you talking about? I haven't done anything wrong. I'm a good boy."

He pressed a steel-toed boot into my chest. "She told me how you been showing up at the club night after night to watch her jiggle. Told me that one night you even followed her home. Said she spotted you climbing up a mesquite tree, trying to get another peek. You're a sick fuck, ain't you, boy?"

I spit out a loose tooth and wiped off some blood with my forearm. "Scarlett is a goddamn liar," I said. "I'm no peeping Tom. I'm an upstanding citizen."

But the ugly son-of-a-bitch didn't believe me. Without fair warning, he swung his leg back and kicked me three

1

times in the side, causing me to fart and spit up bile. Then he squatted down next to me, patted my cheek with the palm of his hand, and said, "Listen to me, you freak. The name is Ponso Arguello, and Scarlett Acres is my property until further notice. So from now on, don't talk to her, don't look at her, don't even think about her. 'Cause next time, I'm not gonna be so gentle. Next time they'll be scraping your face from this here pavement."

He got back to his feet, kicked me one more time for good measure, and strode slowly toward Main Street. With great effort I managed to pull myself to a sitting position. Then I shouted after him. "To hell with you. You're not so bad. You're not so tough. Next time you're gonna wish you didn't mess with Frankie Avicious. 'Cause I'm a mean motherfucker. I know Kung Fu. I know Tae Bo." But Ponso Arguello didn't turn around, didn't even slow down.

Feeling defeated and more than a little bit tired, I lay back down on the asphalt, using a half-eaten rotisserie chicken as a pillow. I stared up at the bone moon and pictured Ponso loving my beautiful Scarlett. And as a filthy breeze washed over my face, I made a promise: one of these days I'd teach that boy a lesson or two.

I slept in my car that night—a monkey-shit-brown Beretta with three missing hubcaps and a rusted hood. I woke myself up by hacking a pint of blood. I pried open my eyelids with my fingers. Everything hurt. I felt as if I'd gone twelve rounds with a hyperactive orangutan, then gotten kicked in the groin by a twelve-year-old girl wearing soccer cleats.

I fumbled for a cigarette, found a soggy one still stuck on my lower lip, and lit it. I sucked down the nicotine, carbon monoxide, tar, cyanide, arsenic, ammonia, and the other four thousand or so chemicals with great relish.

I rolled down the window. Outside, the desert sun was blazing and the air was still. Eight in the morning and it was already hotter than a fireman's scrotum. I wiped the sweat from my forehead, hit the engine, and drove. I turned on the radio, but it was just talk, talk, talk, and that made me good and depressed. It was the usual topics: greed, drugs, and murder. And that was just the sports news.

The slaughterhouse where I worked was a sprawling concrete complex on Route 95 called Sunshine Foods. Steam billowed from smokestacks like a modern-day sacrifice to God. Black ladders zigzagged up the windowless walls. Across the highway from the plant, tagged cattle were packed in the stockyard grazing, blissfully unaware of the savagery that awaited them. Everything smelled like manure, rotten eggs, and burning blood.

The parking lot was filled with beat-up pickups and worn-out cars. I drove slowly to the entrance, a familiar shroud of dread covering my skull. In the booth a fat man was reading a newspaper and didn't bother looking at my ID card when I flashed it to him. He just nodded his head and opened the gate. I parked my car in the back of the lot and turned off the engine. Workers were walking through the parking lot with their heads down, carrying their lunch boxes and thermoses. I got out of the car and shielded my eyes from the sun.

Inside the locker room, a bunch of Sunshine employees were changing into their work clothes. They dressed in silence except for one poor son-of-a-bitch who sat on the bench rubbing his cross and praying in Spanish. Me, I never cared much for prayer. It always seemed an awful lot like begging, and I'd be damned if I was going to get down on my knees and plead to some Devil-God who got a hard-on by seeing me fail.

I opened my locker, and a few dozen cockroaches scurried out looking for a new crack to hide. Then I began dressing. I put on my gloves and chain-mail apron—metal armor that covered my body, gladiator-style. I stuck my hard hat onto my head and tucked my pants into my boots. The factory whistle blew. Hi ho, hi ho, it's off to work we go.

I walked toward my station. The disassembly line was filled with catwalks, conveyer belts, and pipes. Workers with knives and hooks were attacking dangling sides of beef, struggling to tear off as much flesh as possible, while our foreman, Pete Baxter, shouted at them in Spanish, telling them to work faster, faster. About twenty feet in front of them, a burly man with a Paul Bunyan beard stood at the ready with a power saw, waiting for the next skinless steer to chop in half. His goggles were covered with blood and brains. He nodded at me solemnly, as if we were at a funeral. I guess we were. Now the stink was getting bad. I dodged the carcasses swinging from the blood rail like Walter Payton avoiding tacklers. As I reached the next level, I could hear the drum-like sound of cattle being knocked unconscious. Electric knives whirred, peeling flesh off carcasses and decapitated heads, slicing tongues from mouths.

I approached my station, the "sticker" station. In technical terms, my job was to make a vertical incision along the carotid arteries and jugular veins, causing the cow to bleed out so the other workers could safely skin, eviscerate, and split the animal. In not so technical terms, my job was to cut the throat of each and every goddamn cow that set foot in Sunshine Foods.

The early-shift sticker flashed a grin when he saw me. "Okay, amigo, now it's your turn," he said. He finished a final kill before stepping out of line. I quickly took his place. Within seconds the next steer swung my way. I gripped my knife hard and stuck the cow in its neck. Textbook. The blood splattered on my goggles, and I wiped it off with my sleeve. Then, a few seconds later, the next one arrived. I greeted it the same way. Its legs kicked in reflex, and I heard it groan. Eight and a half hours to go. I took a deep breath and looked down at the floor. My boots were submerged in blood.

A few days earlier, some Guatemalan immigrant had gotten pulled into the cogs of a conveyer belt while he was cleaning. No one there knew how to turn off the goddamn machine so they just sat there and watched as his arms and legs and chest and ass were shredded into a bloody mess. The plant was closed for a half day while they pretended to fix the machinery malfunction. This afternoon, Richard Richardson, Director of Operations, was coming to tour the plant and speak to the workers to allay any fears that Sunshine Foods wasn't one hundred and ten percent committed to worker safety.

We had been warned about his arrival and given an updated protocol. While he was here, no cattle were to be legged or skinned alive. If meat dropped on the ground during processing, we were expected to rinse it thoroughly before placing it back on the conveyer belt. Workers were to report immediately if the sewers got clogged up due to coagulated blood or fecal matter. Additionally, there was to be no cursing, laughing, or loud conversation. The line speed would be slowed during Mr. Richardson's visit to make it easier to follow these guidelines. This, they kept reminding us, was a special day.

So work was pretty trouble-free that afternoon. I only had to stick one or two cows per minute and most of them were even unconscious. Big Dick didn't show up until the end of my shift. He was a short man with a large round gut and a red leathery face. His eyebrows looked like gray caterpillars, and his lips resembled bloated sausages. Baxter gave him rubber boots to cover his Italian shoes, but he refused the hard hat, choosing instead to wear his trademark white cowboy hat. A real man of the people.

For twenty minutes or so, he, Baxter, and a group of newspaper photographers walked around the plant, talking and joking with the workers. Dick even used some halting Spanish to speak with the Mexicans. They were undoubtedly impressed.

At some point Baxter led the group to my station. I had just finished a kill. I was about to open up my arms and give Dick a great big bear hug, but before I could, he quickly stuck out his hand and said, "Hi, I'm Richard Richardson, Director of Operations of this here company. What's your handle, son?"

I nodded my head slowly and returned the wink. "Frankie Avicious," I said.

His sausage lips upturned into a grin. "And how long

have you been working for Sunshine Foods?"

"Five short years," I said. "Sped by faster than a cheetah with a firecracker up its ass."

"Then I take it you enjoy your job?"

"Enjoy my job? That's funny, sir. That's very funny. No, sir, I don't enjoy it at all. You see, here at Sunshine we workers are treated nearly as badly as the cattle. The supervisors spend their shifts sticking prods up our asses, figuratively, occasionally literally. The wages stink and so do the carcasses. But you already know that, Dick, and it doesn't bother you one bit. Because for you and all the other sons-of-bitches sitting in your leather recliners, smoking your Cuban cigars, and drinking your fifty-year-old scotch, it's all about the profits, isn't it? Keep that killing line moving, meat is money, to hell with worker safety. Yeah, Dick, I've dislocated my shoulder, broken three fingers, ruptured my spleen, stabbed myself a dozen or more times, lost the will to live. And that was just this morning. You think I enjoy working for your goddamn company? Well, if you believe that, then I've got a nice oceanfront property up my ass for sale."

Or maybe I said, "Yes sir, I enjoy my job very much."

Mr. Richardson patted me on the back. "Yes, Frankie, I've got a good feeling about you. I've got a feeling that you, as much as anybody, know what Sunshine Foods is all about. Sure, it's about the wholesome products we produce and package for this great country of ours on a daily basis. But that's not all. No, Frankie, it's about the people. Good, honest, hardworking folks, like yourself, working together to create a better tomorrow. You may not believe me when I tell you this, son, but we're all in this together. I may have the fancy title, but I'm no different than you, Frankie. And I'm certainly no different than poor Lorenzo Sanchez, who lost his life so tragically yesterday. My heart goes out to him and his family, and I want to assure you and the rest of the dedicated employees that they will be compensated generously for their loss, just as your family would be if, God forbid, something were to happen to you. Because you're the people I go to church with, the people I go to the grocery store with, the people I rub shoulders with. The people, Frankie. The people are the heart and soul of this company, and I aim to keep it that way. You keep up the good work. May God bless you, may God bless Sunshine Foods, and may God bless America."

I nodded my head, thanked him sincerely. The cameras clicked. The next cow came down the line, and Baxter squeezed Big Dick's shoulder and pulled him back. I grabbed a hold of the steer's neck, reached around and stabbed its jugular vein. The blood squirted from its throat and splattered on Dick's cowboy hat. For a moment he seemed stunned. He just stood there, his mouth slightly ajar. Then he removed the hat and tried wiping the blood off with his hands.

"Goddamn it, Avicious," Baxter said. "You're always fucking things up."

But Dick just shook his head and laughed. "Oh, it's no big thing," he said. "I can pick up another one of these any old day. Besides, I think this young man has quite a future in the company. I consider him family."

And I was. You see, Richard Richardson was my father-in-law.

CHAPTER 2

I should tell you about myself, not that you care. I was born and conceived in the same place: the back seat of a piss-yellow '64 Chevy. My parents were decent, God-fearing folks who went to church whenever they weren't too drunk or stoned to crawl out of bed. Dad was a part-time night custodian, part-time auto mechanic, and a full-time bastard. He was as dishonest a man as I've ever known: the kind of fellow who'd pickpocket his own wallet. He also had a hell of a temper, and if he suspected, just suspected, that Mom was being unfaithful, well, he wasn't opposed to pressing a lit cigarette against her thigh, or grabbing her by the ponytail and smashing her pretty face against the coffee table.

I loved my mother the way a son should love a mother, and that's all there is to say about that. The whispers that I heard, the sideway glances, those were just small-minded people looking to stir up resentment. But Dad listened to them, yes he did. And as I became a man, he became more paranoid, more suspicious. Mom and I might go out for a bite to eat, or maybe to a movie, and Dad would sit in the kitchen and drink and drink and wait and wait.

Then Mom got pregnant, and that was a hell of a thing. It could have been anybody—Tim Walker, Jeb Pooley, Pastor Duncan. Maybe even Dad himself. But his brain had been so badly contaminated by the local bacteria that he couldn't think straight. He borrowed Lucky Pincer's bowie knife and carved the word *slut* onto Mom's forehead.

What he did to me was even worse.

When I was fifteen years old, they buried Dad and sent Mom to prison. I moved in with my aunt Rosie. She was a miserable old lady who ate pickled herring by the pound, suffered from frequent asthmatic attacks, and spent her days rearranging a considerable collection of antique dolls. They were all over the house, those creepy sons-of-bitches, just staring at me, waiting for me to sin. There was nowhere I could go to escape their watchfulness, not even the bathroom or my own bedroom. I blame them, along with an increased appetite for whiskey, for the immense amount of anxiety I felt during those years. And that anxiety was my downfall. Because it caused me to act mean. I started getting into fights. Violent fights. They—my aunt Rosie, the school principal, a psychologist—gave me a lot of chances, but I didn't change. Not much anyway. So they put me in a reform school in Casa Grande. Three years later I was convicted of first-degree assault.

I served a nickel's worth. They said I was there to be rehabilitated, but that was just a line. I didn't get better. If anything, I just got meaner and angrier. I made it through, though. What doesn't kill you doesn't kill you.

Two weeks after I was granted parole, I met Ruth Richardson. I was at a little downtown tavern called the Loony Bin, eating cows' tongues and drinking Jagermeister when she sat down next to me. She told me it was her half birthday. I bought her a mai tai. Less than an hour later, I performed cunnilingus on her in the restroom of a Sinclair station. It was love at first sight.

Within a month, Ruth was already talking marriage. Me, I just blew it off. Then I met her old man. He was so goddamn rich that he used twenty-dollar bills to wipe his ass. I figured that I had finally caught a break after a lifetime of crap luck. Without thinking twice, I pawned my soul for an engagement ring and drove her fat ass down to the justice of the peace.

A few weeks after the papers were signed, Richard Richardson handed me a cigar and told me that he'd be more than willing to set me up with a job in his company. Naturally, I was thinking a nice desk job where I'd have a pretty secretary who would pour me coffee and call me "sir" and let me gaze at her round booty as she bent down to pick up a dropped file. Instead, he got me a job inside the rendering plant and later at the slaughterhouse. "A fellow like you—an ex-con, I mean—is lucky to get regular work at all," he said. Lucky. Like hell. I couldn't have gotten a break if I'd smashed my own fingers with a hammer.

Well, after work I was plenty angry. I hadn't expected to be treated that way. So ashamed of his daughter's husband that he had to pretend we were strangers. Couple that with the beating Ponso Arguello had given me, and I was damn near ready to explode.

I climbed into my car and pounded on the steering wheel. It was all wrong. This job, this wife, this life. I straightened up and took a few deep breaths. I knew I needed to do something productive before all the rage and regret boiled over. I started thinking and thinking, trying to figure something out. After mulling through countless possibilities, I finally came to a sensible, albeit not completely original decision. I decided I was going to drive straight to the Big Bust Gentlemen's Club and watch Scarlett Acres take her clothes off.

The club was smoky and seemed silent despite the techno music blasting from the speakers. I quickly scanned the joint for Scarlett's protector, but I didn't see him. A young girl with vacant eyes and badly shaved pubic hair was swaying back and forth on the center stage. An old man with a blond toupee sat alone watching her, a shit-eating grin on his face, a wad of dollar bills in his grubby fist. A couple of mustachioed Mexicans with cowboy hats were sitting at the bar. I sat down next to them and rapped on the counter. A brunette, who was dressed like a stripper but was too old to get paid for it, nodded at me. "What can I get for you, sweetheart?"

"Everclear with a chase of whiskey," I said.

"Six dollars." I gave her five singles and four quarters and told her to keep the change. Then I sucked down my drinks and ordered two more.

It wasn't until nearly seven o'clock that my love took the stage, blowing kisses to all the cockroaches and maggots that were hanging from chairs. Scarlett Acres wasn't much to look at. She had bleach-blonde hair, an acne-scarred face, and a gap between her teeth. Her nose was too big and her ears were too small. About the only thing she had going for her is that she was built a bit lopsided. What I mean by that is she was one hiccup away from giving herself a pair of black eyes.

I found a seat in the corner, concealed by a shadow. I

drank my poison and watched the show. The music was terrible and so was the dancing. Scarlett flopped across the stage and yanked off her clothes with all the grace of a two-bit whore. The set ended. She got down on her knees and hoarded the scattered dollar bills. I got up from my seat and stumbled toward the exit. I knew what time she'd be finishing. And I'd be sitting there waiting for her.

Outside the air was still and the moon looked mean. I leaned against the brick wall. I lit a cigarette and tried to make smoke rings, but I didn't know how. A scorpion scurried across the pavement and I stomped it dead with my boot.

An hour passed, maybe more, before Scarlett appeared through the heat and melancholy. She was wearing a tight pink shirt and a tighter black skirt. She was chewing gum and walking briskly. I didn't know she could do both of them at the same time. She didn't see me until it was too late. I snuck up behind her and grabbed her arm. She shrieked like a stuck pig.

"I've missed you, precious," I said.

"Ow. Let go, Frankie."

"You've got a boyfriend," I said, squeezing harder.

"You...you're hurting me."

"He's a tough guy. Likes sneaking up on innocent drunks. Smashing in their faces."

"I can't control him," she said. "I never told him to do that to you."

"Did it on his own, huh?" I said. "Without any encouragement? You're lying."

"Go home, Frankie. My manager is gonna be coming out the door any minute now and..." I let go of her arm and gave her a nice little shove. She just smirked. "I thought you would have learned by now to leave me alone."

"I'm a slow learner," I said. "I've got the IQ of a corkscrew."

Scarlett fought back a grin. Then she did something that caught me by surprise. She leaned forward and gave me a long kiss on my mouth. There are a thousand different kisses. This one was the kiss of death. "Poor boy," she said. "Lovesick for the wrong girl."

I squeezed my eyes shut and clenched my fists. "One of these days, Scarlett, you're gonna understand. You're gonna understand that you and I are meant for each other, that there's no other way."

"Frankie. I'm just a stripper. I'm not so big into love."

"Then what about your boy Ponso Arguello?"

She shrugged. "What can I say? He's got some money. He buys me nice things."

"And that's all it takes?"

"I'm a shallow person, Frankie. I don't deny it."

The door to the club opened. I could hear the music, but it was muffled, blurry. A man appeared: her manager. Scarlett took a step forward and called for help. I grinned, baring my teeth. "I'll be seeing you," I growled. "And Scarlett, darling, I ain't even close to through with you."

CHAPTER 3

The sign on the edge of town read "Welcome to Huerfano, Arizona, Home of 11,372 Friendly People." I'd lived there damn near half my life and hadn't met but two or three of them. Lost in the desert southeast of Phoenix, Huerfano was your typical Norman Rockwell town—if Norman Rockwell had been an unemployed drug addict. Main Street was littered with boarded-up windows and vacant signs, and the sad-luck neighborhoods were filled with dilapidated bungalows and methamphetamine-fueled desperation. About the only people who stayed in Huerfano were those too scared or too poor to go anywhere else. And hardly anybody ever moved there. Sometimes some Mexicans who got hired at the slaughterhouse or the rendering plant shacked up in the low-income apartments, but even they weren't around for long. Huerfano was a deteriorating town inhabited by deteriorating people.

I drove through town, past the trailer homes, tract houses, and rotting shacks. I crossed over the railroad tracks and through the shadow of an abandoned Texaco station where the gas pumps looked like tombstones. By the time I got home, the sky was in mourning, all black and sad. I parked in the driveway, turned off the engine, and lit a cigarette. The smoke drifted to the ceiling in a crazy gypsy dance.

The porch light was on, but all the lights inside were off. I figured it might be my lucky day. The last person I wanted to see tonight was my wife. The last person I wanted to see any night was my wife. I crushed out my cigarette and shoved open the car door.

Inside the house it was pitch-black, and I had to maneuver around all the clothes, bottles, and pill containers scattered across the floor like an insane asylum rummage sale. I used the walls to guide me until I located the floor lamp. When I turned it on, I nearly lost the Spam and ketchup sandwich I'd had for lunch. Ruth was sitting on a wooden rocking chair, a bottle of Southern Comfort resting on her oversized lap. Her vomit-colored hair was disheveled, mascara was running down her bloated cheeks, and her eyes were bloodshot. In other words, she looked exactly the way she always did.

"How you doin', pumpkin pie?" I asked, bending down to give her a loving peck on the forehead. She didn't answer, so I shrugged and hopscotched across the living room to the kitchen. The dirty dishes were doing an implausible balancing act in the sink. The stink of our house had sobered me up real quickly, so I opened the cabinet and pulled out a bottle of whiskey and a bottle of gin. I grabbed the freshest-looking dirty glass from the sink and poured two-fisted. I took a long gulp, but it didn't taste quite right, so I added a splash of rum. I sat down at the kitchen table and rested my eyes, counting in my head how many seconds of peace and quiet I could enjoy before Ruth would drag me back down to the purgatory that was my life. I made it to thirty-seven.

I heard Ruth's elephant steps crashing on the hardwood floor. I looked up. She was standing in the doorway

with her arms folded. I continued drinking my whiskey/
gin/rum special and staring straight ahead. After several
minutes of foot-tapping and loud sighing, she took a few
steps toward me and stopped. Then the old routine began.
"You've been screwing one of your whores, haven't you,
Frankie?" she said in her whiny voice.

"Ah, Christ, Ruth," I said. "Now why the hell would
you go and say something like that for?"

"It's nearly midnight," she said. "And you smell like
cheap perfume."

"Yeah, well, I've been trying this new cologne out,
seeing how the guys at work would react to it."

"You're a goddamn liar, Frankie."

I shrugged my shoulders. "Believe what you want to
believe. The truth of the matter is I went out for a couple
of brews with some fellows from work. I guess I lost track
of time. When I finally noticed the hour, I rushed home,
looking forward to seeing you, maybe getting a 'Hello,
how was your day, sweetheart?' Something. Instead, I
deal with this. It's a crying shame. Your tycoon father is a
cheapskate, so I have to bust my ass all day to keep food
on the table and a roof over our head. Then I get home
and have to deal with your mean-hearted accusations.
That just ain't right."

And it was true. She had no right accusing me. Why, I
hadn't been unfaithful more than a couple dozen times,
and she'd only caught me red-handed twice. I picked up
my glass and spilled some booze into my mouth, gargling
it for a moment before swallowing. When I looked up,
Ruth's face was buried in her hands, and her shoulders
were rising up and down. I sat there for a good while, not
making any move to comfort her, just watching her

suffer, and frankly enjoying the hell out of it. Finally, I cleared my throat and spoke. "Hey," I said. "There's no need to get so upset now, darling. I wouldn't have ever gone out with my friends if I'd known that you'd get so emotional about it."

She took her hands away from her face. Tears were streaming from her eyes and snot was draining from her nose. She shook her head. "No," she said. "You didn't do anything wrong, Frankie. I mean, if you say you were with your friends, then I believe you."

"Of course I was," I said. "I just needed a little wind-down time, that's all. I know I should have called..."

She bit her lower lip. "I guess that sometimes I just start doubting myself, start doubting us, and I start to wonder why you're still with me when I'm so...so...well, you know."

Yeah. I did know. Fat. The woman had put on so much weight that it looked as if she'd eaten herself. She had more rolls than a bakery and more chins than a Hong Kong phone book. Now, don't get me wrong. If she would've had a domestic skill or two, I might have forgiven her reverse anorexia. But the truth was she cleaned the dishes about as often as a hippo cleans its ass, and the only things she could make in the kitchen were ice cubes and burnt toast. So why was I still with her then? It's a fair question, and I can't say I know the answer for sure. Maybe I was just such a nice guy that I couldn't bear to break her heart in two. Maybe deep down in my soul I really did love and care for her. Maybe. Or maybe I was still with her because her daddy was filthy rich, and I was waiting like a goddamn fool for my big payoff. Take your best guess.

In any case, I continued to play the game. I pulled myself out of the rickety wooden chair and walked across the kitchen to where Ruth was standing. I opened my arms wide—very wide—and pulled her close to me, stroking her hair. "Now come on, sweetheart," I said. "Don't get down on yourself. You know you're the only one for me. I know we haven't been spending a whole lot of time together lately and I haven't been real pleasant to be around, but that doesn't mean I don't love you."

She started crying again, only this time it was more of a happy, relieved sob. "You...you don't think I'm a terrible wife then?" she asked.

"Terrible wife? Heck no. If there's a better one in western Arizona, she hasn't been born yet."

I pulled her tighter and kissed her on the lips. "Now, sugar buns," I said. "When you start thinking thoughts like that, you need to remind yourself that you're just being silly. You're my little teddy bear, and don't you forget it."

So we just stood there in the kitchen, hugging like any happily married couple would, when, without warning, she gasped and pushed me away. Her eyes suddenly got crazy-looking, and her lower lip started quivering. "You've got lipstick on your mouth," she said, her voice rising with each syllable.

I tried looking down, but it's awful hard to see your own mouth—try it sometime—so I just had to take her word for it. That's where Scarlett had kissed me out of pity. "Well, I'll be damned," I said. "I wonder how that got there."

I should tell you now that Ruth suffered from a rare psychological disorder called insanity. The doctors gave her medication to stabilize her moods, but she must have forgotten to take her magic pills that day. In the wink of a con artist's eye, she went from behaving like a loving housewife to a wild-eyed psychopath. "You bastard," she shouted. "You *were* with someone, you unfaithful bastard. Who is she, Frankie? Who's the little whore you've been fucking?" Then she got to her feet and started pounding on my chest the way a nun wails on a schoolchild.

So it was a matter of self-defense. She might have hurt me if I hadn't done something. I grabbed a hold of her shoulder and gave her a good hard shove, knocking her flat on her plump rump. The shove stunned her. She sat there in the middle of the kitchen looking dazed and confused. "And I love you too, you goddamn slut," I said.

That really set her off. She started shouting at me, saying all sorts of mean-spirited half-truths. "Fuck you, Frankie. Fuck you. You're nothing but a drunk, whoring, ex-con who's not smart enough to get a real job. You barely make enough to pay the mortgage on this shit-hole you call a house, and you don't have the ambition to make things better. And not only that, I think you're a faggot. We've never even consummated our marriage, Frankie. I'll bet you weren't with another lady tonight. I'll bet you were fucking your little gay lover. Fucking him right up the ass. Is that what you were doing, Frankie? Were you sticking your pin-dick into the Hershey highway? You fucking faggot. Look at you. You're such a faggot you're just gonna take it. You're gonna take whatever I say. You're not even man enough to stop your own wife from calling you a faggot, you faggot."

By this point she had stumbled to her feet and was

standing just a few inches away from me. Spit was spraying into my face. Please understand that I'd never hit Ruth before, well except for a couple of times, but her steady barrage of insults somehow pushed me over the edge. I shoved her away from me, just enough to get some space, then really laid into her with a right hook. Caught her just below the eye. Now I'd thrown some punches in my day—hell, you don't serve a nickel's worth without laying a few roundhouse rights—but in all my life I don't think I'd ever landed a better blow than this one. My fist vibrated, and she just stood there for a moment—the way a cartoon character remains suspended after walking off a cliff—then her knees gave way, and she collapsed to the floor. I was pretty worked up, so I gave her a couple of kicks in the ribs for good measure. Then I sat down at the table and took out my pack of Marlboros.

I had already finished two cigarettes and had just lit a third when Ruth stirred. At first it was mainly just moans, but soon she managed to rise to her knees and finally struggle to her feet. She looked pretty bad, what with the way her eye was beginning to swell up and all. For a split second I felt kind of ashamed, the way a child feels when he breaks his mother's best dishes. I walked over to where she was wobbling around and said, "Jesus, honey, I didn't mean to hit you that hard. I guess we both lost our tempers a bit and well...I'll say I'm sorry if you'll say you're sorry."

But Ruth wasn't in the mood to exchange apologies. She walked right past me and made her way to the bedroom. A few minutes later she came out lugging a suitcase filled with who knows what; it wasn't filled with my love letters, I can tell you that much. I offered to help her carry the suitcase, but she didn't respond. Hell, she didn't even bother to kiss me good-bye. She just walked out the front door, letting the wind slam it shut behind her. Me, I returned to the kitchen and drank and drank and drank and...

CHAPTER 4

The knocking on the front door woke me from my stupor. I picked my head up and blinked a few times. Spilling a few dozen curse words from my mouth, I rose to my feet and stood there wobbling like a Bozo doll. I waited until my momentum was facing forward, then swerved around the house until I arrived at the front door. I shoved it open with my shoulder. A man stood in the doorway wearing a green seersucker suit and a porkpie hat, his face obscured by the shadows.

"I hate to disrupt your evening, sir, but once you hear what I have to say, you'll be glad I did. I'm selling watches, finely tuned European watches, at a fraction of the usual cost. If I could just have a moment of your time..." He took a step forward into the light. My throat tightened. I remembered that face. Tight pale skin, long hooked nose, cold gray eyes. Some time had passed, but I remembered that face.

"Jack Marteau," I mumbled. "It's been a while."

His eyes narrowed and his thin lips spread into a grin. "Frankie," he said. "Is that you?"

"In the rotting flesh."

"Why, this is quite a coincidence. I haven't seen you since—"

"Since my old man passed on."

He shook his head solemnly. "That sounds about right. Terrible death it was." But as he spoke I swear to God there was a speckle of glee shimmering in his gray eyes.

"Yeah, well, my life's been nothing but a series of kicks to the groin," I said. Then I nodded at his briefcase. "And what about you? Decided to give up the preaching gig, huh?"

Marteau flashed a phony incredulous expression, his eyes and mouth both widening simultaneously. "Give up preaching? Oh heavens, no. It's just that I've incurred some financial difficulties over the years. Wrongful death suits and such. Selling watches helps to pay off the debts. My real job, as you well know, is selling the truth. To those who will listen."

I grunted. "Don't you think it's a little late to be going door to door? It's nearly midnight."

He looked down at his wristwatch and frowned. "Well, I'll be damned. I must have lost track of time."

I sneaked a peek at his watch. The glass was crushed and both hands were missing. Something wasn't right. I hadn't seen him for such a long time. And now he shows up? Now?

"I don't suppose I could come inside for a while and sit down," Marteau said. "I've been on my feet for several hours."

"Why not?" I said. "Misery's a sucker for company."

He removed his hat and stepped inside, the door slamming shut behind him. We walked through the living room toward the kitchen. He sat down at the kitchen table, placing his briefcase in front of him. I leaned against the sink, pulled out a cigarette, and lit it. He looked up and watched me with bemusement. Like a psychiatrist studying his patient. For a while everything was quiet. When he finally spoke, his voice startled me.

"So tell me, Frankie, because I'm very curious. Your mother. Did you ever manage to lick her little snatch?"

"Say again?"

"I asked if you had some liquor or a little snack."

"I thought you said...never mind. I've got rum and whiskey and gin. And to eat we've got olives and mayonnaise. Oh, and some month-old Chinese food."

"Rum would be fine. And the olives. Are they Spanish or Greek?"

"Spanish. Pimento stuffed."

"Perfect."

I poured us both drinks and handed him the jar of olives. Marteau picked up his glass and took a dainty sip. Then he stuck his pinky finger into the jar, stabbed an olive with his sharp fingernail, and removed it. He placed the olive in his mouth, closing his eyes in pleasure as he chewed.

I crushed out my cigarette in the sink and swallowed down some booze of my own. It didn't go down so good. I started hacking. I grabbed a dishtowel to cover my mouth. Outside the lightning flashed, followed by a groan of thunder. When I looked up, Marteau had snapped his briefcase open. Dozens of watches were inside. All of them were cracked and broken. "As you can see, I have timepieces of every style and color. And I sell them at far below the recommended manufacturer's price."

He pulled out a cracked watch from the briefcase and placed it in front of me. "This is a Citizen titanium watch," he said. "Suggested retail is two hundred ninety-nine dollars and ninety-nine cents. Since I can see you're a hardworking man, I'm willing to part with it for one hundred and twenty dollars. What do you say?"

"No thanks."

"Of course, if you are more budget conscious, this finely crafted Timex Dress Ironman is an absolute bargain. Suggested retail of seventy-nine dollars and ninety-nine cents. It's yours for forty dollars." He stuck the watch in my face. It was missing its big hand.

"I'm not interested."

"Okay, okay! Thirty dollars, no questions asked."

"Jesus Christ, you don't give up, do you?"

"Not easily, no."

Then the rain started falling. It sounded like distant gunfire. I couldn't remember the last time it had rained. Seemed like years ago. I gazed out the window. The streetlights reflected off the asphalt.

"It's not fair, is it, Frankie?"

"What's not fair?"

"You've got so much pain in your eyes."

"Yeah, well, things are tough all over."

"You said you were married."

"That's right."

"Tell me about her. I'm curious as to what type of a woman Frankie Avicious would marry."

I shrugged my shoulders. "What's there to tell? Her name's Ruth. Big ol' woman. When she steps on the scale, it says 'one at a time, please.'"

Marteau didn't laugh. I finished my drink and wiped my mouth with my forearm. "The thing is," I said, "she tricked me into marrying her. She made some promises. Promises she couldn't deliver."

"Promises?"

"Yeah. Unspoken ones. See, her daddy's a big wig at Sunshine Inc. He's so rich that even his maids have maids. You figure that when you marry into that kind of wealth, you'll get a piece of the pie. Don't get me wrong. I didn't expect him to give me a toilet made of diamonds or a palace on Easy Street. I just expected...something. Instead, the only two things he's given me are jack and shit. I think he enjoys watching me struggle to make ends meet, and it doesn't bother him a bit that his own daughter is living in near-poverty while he sips Dom Perignon from his ten-gallon hat. He never approved of her marrying me, not from day one."

"What makes you so sure?"

"Oh, the way he talks to me. The way he patronizes me. Like I'm his goddamn plumber or something. See, he wanted Ruth to marry one of his own kind. He wanted her to marry someone who golfed and went to church and voted Republican. He didn't want her to marry some two-bit ex-con who enjoys hot dogs and beer more than caviar and Scotch."

It was strange, me talking to Marteau so openly, but I guess I had some stuff building up inside me. Normally, whenever I explained the dismal facts of my life to the bartenders, hookers, and transients of Huerfano, they just shook their heads and said, "Ain't life a bitch?" or threw me a lifejacket full of rocks. But Marteau understood. At least he seemed to.

Marteau removed another olive from the jar. He chewed methodically before licking his lips with a lizard-like tongue. His slender fingers tightened around his glass. "And what about this other woman? What did you say her name was?"

I looked up quickly. "You talking about Scarlett?"

"That's right. Scarlett."

"How the hell do you know about her?"

He tapped the table with his fingernails and grinned. "You told me about her, Frankie, don't you remember?"

"No, I—"

"Do you love her?"

"That's a hell of a question."

"And?"

"She reminds me of somebody. Somebody from a long time ago."

Marteau laughed. "Beautiful. An Oedipus complex."

"A what?"

"Nothing, Frankie, nothing. So what's stopping you from sweeping this Scarlett off her feet? What's stopping you from stealing her heart and running away from here, far, far away from here?"

I grunted. "For one, she's got a big ugly boyfriend. And for another, she doesn't seem to like me much."

Marteau stroked his chin and frowned. "That surprises me, Frankie. You're such an original."

"With your compliments and a two-dollar bill, I could get a blow job from a toothless whore."

"Wonderful, Frankie. See what I mean? Such an original."

I took a long swallow of booze and grimaced. "But here's the thing. This Scarlett, she's got a nose for money, mister. If only Ruth's old man wasn't so goddamn greedy and narcissistic..."

Marteau nodded his head sympathetically. He placed his hand on top of mine. His fingers were cold as ice.

"All of this. It makes you enraged, doesn't it, Frankie?"

"Well, I don't like to whine and complain—"

"Oh, please. Considering the obvious inequities you've been forced to face, you seem remarkably restrained. You've been handed a raw deal, Frankie, and you deserve better."

"I suppose I do."

I finished my rum. I was beginning to feel dizzy. Was Marteau dropping something in my drinks? He gathered up his busted watches and placed them in his briefcase.

"So tell me, Frankie, what are you going to do about all of this?"

I stuck a cigarette in the corner of my mouth but didn't light it. "Don't figure there's much I can do."

"Nonsense," he said. "What do you know about cockroaches?"

I didn't think I'd heard him right. "Cockroaches?"

"Mmmm. I know it must sound strange, Frankie, but I greatly admire the cockroach. A most misunderstood, yet resourceful animal. Resourceful enough to survive for four hundred million years. Think about that for a moment. They were here when the continents were formed, remained during the appearance and disappearance of the dinosaur, and watched from the forests of the tropics as monkey-like primates evolved into *Homo sapiens.*"

"Interesting but—"

"Did you know, Frankie, that cockroaches can hold their breath for forty minutes?"

"I can't say that I did, no."

"And that a cockroach can live a week without its head? Can you imagine? The roach only dies because of thirst. Meanwhile, it can live a full month without food. A cockroach also has more than one brain. They can learn to navigate complicated mazes after only four or five attempts. Fascinating creatures, aren't they?"

"That's one word for them."

"And we should take our lessons from these magnifycent creatures of God. When cockroaches are threatened by other insects, they don't back down. Instead, they stalk around in circles, raise their bodies high off the ground and bite and kick until their foe finally retreats. And if their enemy does not surrender, cockroaches have been known to attack and tear off body parts until the other creature dies."

"Jesus Christ," I said. "A little explicit, don't you think?"

Marteau bowed his head and released a petite belch. "I apologize, Frankie. I only wish to point out that survival often means being proactive."

I lit the cigarette that was dangling in my mouth and squinted. "I've been plenty proactive," I mumbled.

He grinned thinly. "Please don't kid yourself, Frankie."

I glared at him, then shook my head slowly. Outside, a car came speeding around the corner, bass pumping, beer bottles crashing on the asphalt. Some dogs howled in protest. A slow wave of depression rose up inside me. "This fucking town," I said. "This fucking life."

"Now, let's not start feeling sorry for ourselves," Marteau said. "That's counterproductive. We need to think pragmatically. Let me ask you a question. Your father-in-law, is he a healthy person?"

I turned and faced him. "Healthy?"

"No dire medical issues?"

"No. But why—"

"Your father-in-law has made his fortune off the backs

of working people like you. He chews you up and spits you out. All so he can live in his mansion and eat his caviar and drive his fancy car. He's a man of questionable character."

"What the hell are you getting at?"

"Certainly you deserve better, Frankie. Certainly you've waited your turn."

The old man crossed his legs and leaned forward. For a moment, the way he maneuvered into the light, it appeared that his gaunt face was on fire. I closed my eyes and gritted my teeth. When I reopened them, Marteau's face seemed to have no form. Instead there were just parts. A nose and a mouth and couple of eyes and some skin and...

I squeezed my glass so hard that it shattered in my hand. "I'm not killing anybody," I heard myself say.

Marteau laughed harshly and feigned surprise. "Who said anything about killing?"

"I know I'm not the best guy in the world. I whore around. I lie. I cheat. I've got a nasty mean streak. But murder? I won't do it."

Marteau snapped closed his briefcase and glanced at his broken watch. "Oh Lord, look at the time," he said. "I really must be going. I've got a meeting with a pro-spective client."

"I'm not killing anybody," I mumbled again.

He laughed and muttered something under his breath. It sounded like "You just wait and see."

CHAPTER 5

Somehow I made it to work the next day. It was brutal. The line was just smoking. Every other steer was arriving at my station alive and kicking. I complained to Baxter about it, but he told me to stop bitching, that the cows were fucking dead and the kicks were just "death reflexes." But I'll tell you this much: it would have been a hell of a trick if those cattle were dead, because most of them were still mooing and rolling their eyes when I tried slashing them.

See, the problem was with the knocker. He was this illegal who didn't speak a word of English and didn't look older than sixteen. His lone job was to knock the cattle unconscious by shooting them in the head with a re-tractable steel bolt. But they hadn't trained him properly, and he wasn't hitting the steers squarely. He'd shoot five, six times or more, and the cattle would still be kicking. Since we had to keep the lines moving, the shacklers usually went ahead and chained up the cattle even though they weren't unconscious. By the time they reached me, they were as hyped up as Chihuahuas on speed. I couldn't get a good stick, and they weren't bleeding out properly. Meanwhile, the leggers and skinners were getting pissed because it's not easy to clip legs and skin heads of live cows. They were cursing at me and shouting, "Stick those motherfuckers!" In a polite way, I told them to shut the fuck up, that it wasn't my fault, that it was the goddamn knocker, but those pricks didn't want an explanation, they just wanted the cattle dead, and didn't we all?

This one steer was particularly tough. Even after having being shot by the retractable gun, stuck in the neck, and having its legs cut off, the beast was still ready to brawl. When the head skinner started peeling the flesh off its skull, the cow began making the most awful bellowing sound you've ever heard. Watching and listening to that steer being tortured made me feel anxious. I tried taking deep breaths, but the anxiety kept building. I needed it to stop.

I left my station and walked over to where the cow was stubbornly struggling for life. Without pause, I grabbed a rotted two-by-four and started beating the cow over the head. See, I just wanted to put the goddamn animal out of its misery. I pounded and pounded until the board finally shattered. I threw the broken pieces onto the ground. But was the cow dead? Hell no. This legless skinless steer with a broken skull kept right on fighting. Bring it on, Avicious, bring it on! The anxiety got worse. I looked around frantically for an object, any object. The only thing I could find was a water hose. I pinned down the cow with my knees and shoved the hose up its nose. Then I walked over to the faucet and turned it on full blast. That did the trick. The cow gurgled, twitched, and died.

Of course, the other workers were watching me the whole time, just laughing and cheering. The head skinner shouted, "Avicious's lost it! The cows have finally gotten to him."

I turned off the hose and spit on the ground. Baxter

appeared. When he saw the mutilated cow lying on the cement, he just shook his head and grinned. "Get back to your station, Avicious. Meat is money, you crazy son-of-a-bitch."

After work I felt good and depressed. I needed a drink. Goddamn it, I needed a drink. Tucker's Tavern was across the highway from the plant, where all the meat-packers gathered. It was nothing special, just a little hole in the wall with a jukebox that always played country music, and a pool table covered with tattered blue felt. License plates from various states and years covered the walls. Bud and whiskey were the drinks of choice here; nobody ever ordered a cosmopolitan, that's for sure. Occasionally a decent-looking lady would show her face, and man, it was like sharks at a feeding frenzy.

On this particular evening, the bar was pretty crowded. Johnny Cash was singing about shooting a man in Reno. Three young Mexicans holding pool sticks were arguing about something. In the middle of the bar, a couple of gorillas were trying to carry their very drunk, very fat buddy to the front door. He kept mumbling about some whore he'd banged in Tucson. I pushed my way through the crowd. I noticed a few fellows from my shift sitting in a corner booth. I nodded at them but sat by myself at the bar. I guess you could say I've always been a bit of a loner. I like people just fine, but I've never had much use for them.

The bartender was a thick guy with a crew cut, a scraggly goatee, and a tattoo of a python on his forearm. He'd probably served me a hundred times or more, but he never showed any signs of recognition. He had all the personality of a doorknob. I ordered some tequila and a pint of Drain-O as a chaser. I drank one or two or a dozen. My exhilaration disappeared as quickly as the liquor, replaced by that familiar sense of dread. And as my head slumped to the counter, the memories started rattling around in my skull...

The cheap motels. The neon lights. The empty laugh tracks on the television. The sad smiles. The desperate promises. The nasty fights. The warm kisses. And the endless waiting. *"There's no escape for us, Frankie. They'll find us sooner or later. We can't run forever..."*

I rose to my feet. I didn't feel so good. The stink from the town was filling up the bar, causing my head to spin. I went to the bathroom and vomited blood into the sink. Out of the corner of my eye I saw my repulsive reflection in the mirror. I turned away and faced the door, my arms hanging limply at my sides. Then a sudden rage rose through my body. In one abrupt motion, I turned and slammed the mirror with my open palm. The mirror shattered, and for a moment the world was reflected the way I saw it, fragmented and warped.

A skinny man with a bolo tie entered the bathroom, saw all the broken glass and said, "What the fuck happened here?" I pushed him out of the way.

As I staggered out of the bar, the floor had become the ceiling, the ceiling had become the wall, the walls were on fire, and the jukebox wasn't playing anymore. Once outside, I vomited my life's savings into the gutter. Then I wiped my mouth clean with my sleeve and pulled myself up by my hair.

I made my way back toward my car. I tried about six

keyholes before I found the right one. I was too drunk to drive. Hell, I was too drunk to shit myself. But I crawled into my car anyway, hit the engine, and weaved out of the parking lot like a boxer who's gone one round too many.

Crooked thoughts staggered through my brain. "Certainly you deserve better," Marteau had said. Of course I did. I drove and drove. And somewhere between Main Street and my driveway, I made a decision: I wasn't going to wait for opportunity to knock; I was going to squeeze it by the goddamn colon.

The next day I made a few calls. I was curious about an old cell mate of mine. I tracked down his address from his mother. "Tell that rotten son-of-a-bitch he owes me seven hundred and sixteen dollars," she said in a voice crippled by emphysema.

Ty Weaver lived in a bad part of town. Even the rapists and murderers rolled up their windows and locked their doors when driving through. But I had some business I figured he could help me out with. I parked my car in front of a fire hydrant, stepped outside, and wiped the perspiration from my forehead. The sun was dropping beneath the desert floor. I was feeling good and ornery. Some kids were playing catch with a red rubber ball, and it got loose from them. I retrieved it, told them to find another fucking playing field, and booted it down the street. This filthy little girl with dirty blonde pigtails glared at me with hateful eyes before chasing after her precious ball. I pulled out a cigarette and lit it.

The inside of the apartment building was dark and smelled like urine. The walls were covered with graffiti.

"God is love" was written neatly in orange marker. Beneath that "God can suck my white cock."

I walked down the hall until I found apartment six. I rapped on the door a few times and waited. I heard footsteps, then a gravelly voice say something I didn't understand. Moments later, the door opened and a man with acne-scarred skin and a thick goatee opened the door. He wore an A-frame undershirt. On his right arm was a tattoo that said "Don't Tread on Me" beneath a giant red cobra. On his left cheek were three tattoo tears.

He nodded at me, his face remaining expressionless. "Long time no see," he said. "How'd you find me?"

"I called your mom. She sends her regards. Mind if I come in?"

He shrugged. I followed him inside. His apartment was small and cluttered. An American flag hung on the back wall. And beneath the American flag a Confederate flag. On the far wall was a glass case, and inside were dozens of antique guns and what appeared to be an old grenade. The other wall was covered with dead animal heads: a deer, a bull, and a ram.

"Sit down," he said.

I sat down on a dirty gray couch and felt the springs pressing against my ass. He sat down across from me in a creaky wooden chair. He pulled out a package of Red Man chewing tobacco and offered me some. I shook my head. He stuck a big wad into his mouth and swallowed down the juice.

"The last time I saw you, you were shacked up with some redhead," I said.

"You talkin' about Carly?"

"Yeah. You still dating her?"

"Nah."

"Good. No offense, Ty, but that chick was ugly as sin."

"None taken."

"Whatever happened to her anyway?"

"I married her."

I grimaced. "Hey, that's great. That's really great."

He stuck some more Red Man in his mouth. "What do you want, Frankie?"

"I just wanted to catch up on old times, that's all."

"What do you want?" he said again.

I cleared my throat. "I need a gun," I said. "I'd go buy one, but considering my record—"

Ty raised his eyebrows but didn't say anything.

"A couple of weeks ago somebody tried breaking into my house. Nearly scared the old lady to death. I chased him away with a baseball bat, but it got me to thinking. This world is a dangerous place, and no sense in pushing my luck. Next time I want to be ready. Next time I want to be able to blow away that son-of-a-bitch."

Ty nodded in sympathy. "Did you get a good look? Probably one of those goddamn Mexicans. Damn wet-backs are taking over this town."

"Yeah, I think it was a Mexican, come to think about it. Or it might have been a Canadian. It was kind of dark."

"What makes you think I've got a gun?" Ty asked. "I'm a felon just like you."

I looked around the room. "Just a hunch."

Ty yawned. His teeth were black, but his mouth was empty. He must have swallowed all the chewing tobacco. His eyes focused on me, and he nodded his head. "You're damn lucky I owe you a favor."

As far as I could recall I'd never done a thing for him, but I didn't bother correcting him. He walked to the back of the living room and opened a door I hadn't noticed was there. He closed it behind him, and I remained on the couch alone.

When Ty returned, he was carrying a black .45. He cocked it, aimed it at my head and pulled the trigger. "TSW pistol series," he said. "Law enforcement model. Double action. Made of aluminum alloy. Make a Mexican's head explode like a grape."

"I like grapes," I admitted.

He got me some ammunition, "enough to last you a good while," and handed me the gun. "Do me a favor," he said. "Don't tell anybody where you got this from. Understand?"

"Quiet as a shell-shocked mime," I said and got up to leave. He grabbed a hold of my shoulder.

"We're even now," he said. "Don't come back here no more."

"We're even," I repeated and walked out the door.

When I got outside, I saw that my car had a brand-new parking ticket stuck on the windshield. The girl with dirty pigtails appeared out of nowhere, bouncing her rubber ball and grinning. "Serves you right," she said. "You're a mean man."

CHAPTER 6

I paid Scarlett Acres a visit. She lived next to the railroad tracks in a little pink bungalow. An American flag hung from the house, snapping to attention in the summer breeze. A black Lab lay on the porch. I couldn't tell if it was dead or sleeping. I parked my car, one tire on the sidewalk, and stepped outside.

I walked across the lawn, dodging dog crap and used condoms. The Labrador lifted its head and growled at me halfheartedly. I stood on the porch and looked in the front window, shielding the glare with my hand. Scarlett was sitting on the couch in panties and a T-shirt, watching television. *Dr. Phil*, I think. I like Dr. Phil. He forces me to confront my problems. I pounded on the window with the palm of my hand. Scarlett looked up. When she saw me, she frowned. I have that effect on women. I held up one finger indicating that I would only take a single moment of her time, but she shook her head. "Go away," she mouthed. I rapped on the window again, this time doing the Running Man dance. After thinking it over for a moment, Scarlett rose to her feet and marched to the front door, her bleach-blonde hair a matted mess. She opened the door a crack and said, "You trying to charm me?"

"Yeah. Is it working?"

"Not so far. What do you want?"

I took a step forward, peering over her shoulder. The living room was decorated tastefully, with paintings of unicorns and mermaids and Fabio. I pulled back my greasy hair with my hand. "I've got some money coming my way," I said. "This is confidential information, so please treat it as such."

A nasty grin appeared on Scarlett's face. "Is this the same old story about your tycoon father-in-law?"

"As a matter of fact, it is. But this time I've got it all figured out. It's a done deal. Just give me a few weeks. You and me, we're gonna run away from here and never look back. You ever been to New England?"

She shook her head. "I've never even been out of Arizona."

"I'll tell you what we'll do. We'll find us a friendly little town with white-spire churches and tree-lined streets. We'll get ourselves a big ol' Victorian with a fireplace, and sit on the porch and watch the world pass us by. There'll be no slaughterhouses, no manure odors, no bar fights, no train whistles blowing, no Spanish cursing, no strip clubs. At night we'll look up in the sky and see a million stars shining like untouched diamonds..."

For a moment anyway, the cynicism seemed to fade from Scarlett's eyes. But then the sneer reappeared. "Why do you like me so much, Frankie?" she said. "I'm nothing special."

"You're special to me," I said. "Listen. Right now I'm a card-carrying member of the underclass, the kind of guy people go out of their way to spit on even if their own dicks are on fire. A guy that's been stepped on so often his guts are spilling out of his ass. But when I see you, when

I'm with you, everything's different. You give me hope. You give me a reason to believe. I can't explain it. Not rationally. But I have faith that somewhere in that heart of yours, buried deep in a ventricle, there's a place for poor old me."

Scarlett opened her mouth, but there was no sound. Then she opened it again. "Frankie. I...I..."

"Stay where I can find you," I said. "It won't be long till I come knocking again. And then everything's gonna be the way it should. You just wait and see."

With a tip of a nonexistent hat, I spun around and waltzed across the lawn, a melody of love looping in my brain. As I reached my car, I glanced back at the porch. Scarlett was still there watching me, her hair swaying in the breeze.

Over the next few days I didn't do a hell of a lot. I watched television, ate Doritos, and drank more than a dehydrated fish. I barely slept. A few times I drove out among the cacti and coyotes and practiced shooting my gun. I wasn't Billy the Kid or anything, but considering how much my hands shook, I wasn't terrible. I could hit an oversized saguaro from short range, anyway.

And then came July fourteenth.

The morning was like any other. I woke up early. I took a long, hot shower. I ate breakfast. I read the paper. There were lots of stories about the war in Iraq. Americans were dying, and the world was going to hell. It didn't matter. I had my own problems to think about.

I left the house at eight fifty-two. The sun was already sizzling in the blank blue sky. Hot weather breeds insanity.

I found a country music station on the radio. Hank Williams was singing. Talk about a lonesome voice. Jesus H. Christ. Enough to make a grown man cry. I drove along little-used dirt roads and back highways surrounded by bur sage, cholla, prickly pear, and saguaros. Other than an occasional derelict stucco cottage, there were no signs of human life. I pulled out a cigarette and rested it between my lips. I glanced at my face in the rearview mirror. I didn't like what I saw.

Dick Richardson's modest little home was located on the edge of town, nestled on a hillside overlooking the slaughterhouse. It was an eleven thousand three hundred-square-foot house with eight bedrooms, six bathrooms, a large flagstone patio with Mediterranean landscaping, a built-in barbecue, an in-ground Jacuzzi, a recreation room, a wet bar, a parlor, a study, a theater, a butler's pantry, a grand chef's kitchen with a Viking range and Bosch double ovens, a master suite furnished with a one hundred-inch Sony home theater, and an open living area with high ceilings, granite floors, Hunter Billas silhouette blinds, Casablanca fans, walls of cherry shelves, and a winding marble staircase.

I parked at the bottom of the hill in a little clearing covered by palo verde and mesquite trees. I killed the engine and sat there for a few moments, staring through the dirty windshield at the nothingness in the distance. I got out of the car and slammed the door shut. Then I stuffed the gun in the front of my Wrangler carpenter jeans. A hot breeze was blowing, kicking up dirt and an old Snickers candy bar wrapper. I made my way up the hill, stopping every few steps to catch my breath and light a new cigarette. By the time I reached the top, I was sweating like a fat man in long johns running a marathon in the Sahara Desert with an orangutan hanging from his neck.

I wiped my forehead with my sleeve and stamped out my cigarette. The metal of the gun felt good against the skin of my stomach. I took a deep breath and rang the doorbell. For a few moments there was just silence; then I heard some footsteps on the hardwood floor and saw Dick Richardson and his dried-out sausage lips peering through the frosty window. He opened the door. He was wearing a white bathrobe with his initials on it. "Frankie, ol' pal," he said. "How you been?"

"Fine," I said. "Real good."

He gave me a hearty handshake and a pat on the back. He made no mention of our last meeting at the slaughterhouse. "Some hot weather we've been having, huh?"

I nodded my head. "Well, you know what they say. If you don't like the weather in Arizona, just wait a couple million years and it's bound to change."

His bloated sausage lips spread into a grin. "Ain't that the truth, Frankie, ain't that the truth."

I followed him inside. Music was playing. Barry Manilow. He led me into the living room. I sat down on the red leather couch and looked around. The ceilings were vaulted and the walls were filled with dramatic artwork including a near-life-sized painting of the Last Supper. A bleach-blond Jesus sat at the middle of the table with his arms raised, while the disciples looked on in awe. The table was filled with good food, like bread and wine and hamburgers.

"Can I get you something to drink?" Dick said. "Figure you to be a brewskie man."

"Actually, I'm not much of a drinker," I said.

"I admire that in a man."

"Of course, I wouldn't want to be rude, so I guess I'll try one or two."

"Now you're talking, partner."

Dick Richardson disappeared into the kitchen. I pulled out my .45 and rested it on my lap. Suddenly I felt very tired. I closed my eyes for a moment. I thought about how life sure is funny. The very things you need to make yourself happy, truly happy, are always just out of grasp. God uses those things like rabbits at a greyhound race, forcing us to run faster and faster with the never-ending illusion of the grand payoff.

Mr. Richardson appeared a moment later with a couple of glasses of beer. He saw my pistol but acted like it was a child's toy. "What are you doing with that, partner?" he laughed.

I looked down and shook my head. I sighed deeply and rose to my feet, the pistol now dangling from my hand. "You should've kept your doors locked, mister," I said. "You take your chances letting an ex-con into your house."

"Frankie," he said, the smile vanishing. "What...What do you want?"

I walked slowly, methodically, across the room. I flipped the gun in my hand so that I was gripping the barrel. "What do I want, huh? That's a hell of a question, Dick, a hell of a question. Where should I start? First, I want to know that my vote counts when electing a president. The Electoral College is antiquated, don't you think? I mean, if I vote for candidate A, but candidate B wins the state, then my vote no longer counts. Candidate B gets all the electoral votes from my state. That's not a true democracy, sir. That's what James Madison referred to as 'the tyranny of the majority.' Incidentally, did you know that as a convicted felon, I'm not even allowed to vote? Yeah, even though I've served my time, paid back my debt to society, I'm completely excluded from the process. It's just not right.

"Second, I want universal health care. It's a crying shame that the most prosperous nation in the world allows such a high percentage of its children and elderly to suffer without proper treatment. We need to stand up to the big insurance and drug companies that lead to soaring premiums. Did you know that over the past several years, premiums have risen four times faster than wages? That's unacceptable. That's not the American way.

"Third, I think we need to invest in our schools. Too often our nation's schools are not given the proper resources to succeed. Today's children are tomorrow's doctors, lawyers, educators, and custodians. Instead of wasting our money on ineffectual government programs and obsolete defense systems, we should be focusing on making our public education system the envy of all countries.

"And fourth," I paused savoring the buildup to the biggest moment of my life, "I want what is owed me. You've had your fun. Now it's time that I have mine." Before Dick Richardson could react, I swung my hand brutally, smashing the side of his face with the butt of the gun. The beers dropped from his hands and the glass shattered against the hardwood floor. Stunned, he staggered backward and leaned unsteadily against the wall.

"It didn't have to be like this," I explained. "I gave you a chance. But you people. You fucking people."

He whimpered pathetically, his face now a mess of

blood, tears, and terror. He shook his head spastically. "Frankie. Son. Please. I'll give you money. I can write you a check. Name your price."

I shook my head. "It's too late for that, Dick."

I took another step forward, and he slid down against the wall until he was squatting on the floor. His hands tightened into fists, and he stared at me with frantic eyes. "You need to pray, Frankie," he said. "Jesus will answer your prayers. You just have to pray hard enough. He never turns his back on anybody no matter what his sins."

"I'm no beggar," I said.

"You're a good man," he said. "I know you are. You come from good family."

I shook my head somberly. Then I raised the gun and cocked it. Closing one eye, I aimed it directly at his chest where his heart would have been. Instinctively, he shielded his face with his arms. My fingers tensed and the trigger gave. A deafening explosion filled the room. Blood seeped through his robe, just below his collarbone. I took another step forward and fired once, twice, three times at his twitching body. Then I watched as he died in a puddle of blood and beer and broken glass.

I went back to the couch and sat down. I laid the gun gently on a satin pillow. The sun shone through the curtains, and everything was orange.

CHAPTER 7

It was a botched burglary, that was plain to see. Probably a drifter, a fellow with a long record who couldn't bear the thought of going back to the big house. When Richard Richardson had appeared unexpectedly, he had panicked, shot him dead...

Once news hit of the homicide, there was much alarm in the picture-perfect town of Huerfano, Arizona. After all, Richard Richardson was a well-respected, God-fearing community member, and if he could be butchered so inhumanely, well who would be next? So the local authorities started a spirited manhunt, reassuring the towns-folk that their tormenter would be brought to justice.

Unfortunately, with little manpower and resources, the investigation soon slowed and then ceased. The murderer had probably hopped a train, and he could have been anywhere—Pueblo, Colorado; Topeka, Kansas; Rockford, Illinois; Allentown, Pennsylvania; Tallahassee, Florida; besides, the public's attention span is short, and it didn't take long for them to forget about the brutal slaying. Soon they were back to living their meaningless lives: taking out the trash, emptying the dishwasher, folding the laundry, screwing the wife, walking the dog, sweeping the floors, beating the kid. The drifter had vanished into the great void of our consciousness.

CHAPTER 8

I got to work in the master bedroom, flipping over mattresses, yanking up rugs, and pulling out drawers, adding a bit of authenticity to the scene of the crime. After leaving the master bedroom, I continued my rampage in the living room, the parlor, and finally the kitchen, pausing only long enough to guzzle some Dom Perignon and gobble some caviar. I'd never tried either before, and I liked them plenty, believe me. I'd always had expensive tastes, with the exception of my women, clothes, and the company I kept. Anyway, by the time I was through with the house, it looked as if an epileptic pit bull had taken up residence there.

As I wandered through the hallways, a wave of sadness descended upon me. Not the depressed kind of sadness that I got after drinking heavily, but the nostalgic kind. Never again would I set foot in this house, never again would I see Dick Richardson alive. It was the end of an era, I guess. He didn't deserve to live, but it was still difficult to comprehend that he was gone.

I exited the house and hurried down the long winding hill until I came to my car. I glanced at my watch. It was eleven-eighteen. The sun was shining hateful as ever, and perspiration was dripping into my eyes, making them sting. I got in the car and just sat there for a while. Then I hit the engine and drove.

I drove for some time, trying to clear my mind. Somehow, I ended up at Sunshine Foods, that redbrick-veneered madhouse. The smoke rose from the roof like the whole fucking building was ready to explode. And I wished it would.

I got out of the car and sat on the hood. I lit a cigarette and closed my eyes. In the past, I'd allowed the meanness of the world to get the better of me, allowed it to strip away all hope and dignity. But now things had changed. No longer was I dragging my broken spirit through this broken town. I'd finally fought back.

I opened my eyes. A bearded worker exited the slaughterhouse. I recognized him but didn't know his name. He walked with a limp, his eyes staring at the pavement. I wanted to shout out to him, "Hey buddy, wake up! You're dying, can't you see that you're dying? Every day they're robbing you of your soul, just taking enough so you don't notice. But one day you're gonna wake up and you're not gonna be there anymore. There'll just be a worn-out jalopy of a body with nobody left to drive it.

"But it doesn't have to be like that. This is America, land of opportunities. All you've got to do is pick yourself up by the bootstraps and dust yourself off. With a little elbow grease and inspiration you can be ANYTHING YOU WANT TO BE. Hey brother, I used to be just like you. A walking zombie. But then I realized that changes needed to be made. And look at me now. I'm the real fuckin' deal."

With a wide grin, I crushed out my cigarette and stepped back into the car. I hit the engine and skidded onto the highway. Stepping heavy on the gas, I got her going seventy, eighty, ninety miles per hour. I stuck my arm out the window and pumped my fist. "Don't mess with me!" I shouted. "Ya'll hear? Don't mess with Frankie Avicious!"

The next day I woke up early, ate a nutritious breakfast consisting of all five food groups, and took an invigorating jog as the dazzling sun rose above the picturesque desert saguaros and flora. When I returned, my sleeping beauty was waking from her slumber, and I kissed her delicate forehead as she smiled dreamily. Then we danced to Debussy as the curtains swayed gently in the summer breeze. Well, not quite. Actually, I woke myself up by hacking up some blood. I stumbled out of bed, poured myself a shot of the sixth food group, and proceeded to vomit my remaining happiness into the kitchen sink. We all have routines. I performed my daily regimen of exercise (one push-up, one sit-up, run in place for ten to fifteen seconds) as my body whimpered in protest.

I went to the bathroom to shave. There was no shaving cream left, so I used toothpaste instead. My face was plaque free. When I was done, I gazed at my mug. I forced a grin. "Hello, day," I said. "How are you?"

"Why, I'm just fine, Frankie, thanks for asking. You look rather dapper if I do say so myself."

"Thank you. I try to be meticulous in my appearance, you know."

"Of course. And what do you have planned today?"

"Interesting that you should ask. I'm on my way to work as usual. Only today is a very special day."

"Yeah? Do tell."

"Today is the last day Frankie Avicious does the devil's

work. And he's going out with a bang!"

"That's the spirit, Frankie! Atta boy!"

So here's how the day proceeded: I got to work more than a little bit late and more than a little bit drunk. Pete Baxter, the foreman, was waiting for me with his usual hellfire. "Who the fuck do you think you are showing up late, Avicious?" he shouted. "Who the fuck do you think you are?" His face was bright red, and a vein bulged from his scrawny neck. I imagined drawing my knife and peeling that meanness right off his face. But the violent fantasy only lasted for a moment. I took a deep breath, patted Baxter on the back, and said, "I apologize. I had a bad case of diarrhea this morning. Must have used up seven rolls of toilet paper. Never knew I was so full of shit. Can't you see my eyes aren't brown anymore?"

Baxter didn't think it was funny, but he let it pass. "Get dressed before I find myself a new sticker."

I gave him a quick salute. "Yes, sir! At your command, sir!" Then I raced toward the locker room, a dedicated worker bee trying to make my company and country proud.

Once I was inside the locker room, I decided my company and country could wait a few minutes. I sat down on a bench and leaned against a locker. I pulled out a pint of gin from my boot, a cigarette from my shirt pocket, and thought about Dick Richardson. May he be getting a blow job from Christ himself. I looked up. A Mexican kid was sitting on the bench opposite me. He shook his head in disgust and said something in Spanish, so I said something back to him in French: Fuck you and the cow you rode in on. He left.

After getting my fill of booze and nicotine, I felt

drowsy. I hadn't been sleeping well lately on account of all the nightmares I'd been having. I yawned and lay down on the bench. No sense in rushing into anything. From now on, I decided, I would take things slooooow, take a little time for myself like they do in Europe and in coffee commercials. I slept for a while. I dreamt that I was dreaming of Scarlett. Then I woke up. I stretched, got to my feet, and put on my armor. I sharpened my knife, mindful that dull knives were the number-one cause of injury at Sunshine Foods, where the customer comes first and quality means something.

Eventually I strolled down the killing line, tiptoeing past Baxter to avoid another confrontation. I got to my station. Luis Rivera, the night sticker, was pissed as hell that I was so late, but I lied and told him I'd set him up with some methamphetamine to make things up to him. After that he didn't seem so angry.

I had a pretty good time that morning. Yeah, there was a lot of muck sloshing through my brain, but instead of making myself miserable, I focused on the task at hand: killing, killing, killing. There's no better stress release than slaughtering cattle.

At lunch break, I went to the bathroom, took a fluorescent yellow piss and a gin-tinged vomit. Then I washed my hands in the sink. Five, ten minutes of scrubbing. I even used a Brill-O pad. The red faded, but I couldn't get the smell off. Death covered my hands. I ate lunch (more gin) and returned to the killing line.

Shortly before my shift was over, I began making certain preparations. While Baxter was taking one of his fifteen cigarette breaks, I managed to loosen the overhead shackle wheel that held the chain in place. I gave it just enough slack so it might accidentally jump off the rail if a cow was moving around too much. Then I searched for the ideal steer. At a quarter till four, I found her. She was a big ol' heifer who had taken several shots from the knocker without going down. When she arrived at my station, her eyes were open, blood was trickling from her nose, and I could tell she was pissed. Instead of aiming for her throat, I began stabbing the heifer in the shoulder and face. That got her nice and wild. She flailed and thrashed. She slowed down for a moment, but a quick jab in the belly got her going again. You should have heard that bitch moan and bellow. Just then, according to plan, the shackle wheel came loose. As soon as the other workers heard that sound, they scattered like monkeys: climbing up ladders, diving under tables. In a moment of utter surrealism, the steer broke free from its chain and came crashing down to the floor fifteen feet below. Thud! For several moments, she was still, and all the workers were quiet. But then, like a bovine Christ, she rose from the dead. With agonizing effort, the cow got to her feet and began moving. At first she was just limping along, bellowing in pain, but as she gained determination, she began jogging, then galloping down the corridor, pausing only long enough to knock over an old mustachioed Mexican worker.

I was mighty proud of that steer. Reminded me of myself in some ways. Stubborn and relentless. Yeah, I knew she'd never get away. I knew eventually they'd catch up and shoot her dead. I knew freedom was nothing but fool's gold. I knew all that. But I also knew I had to follow. During the ensuing commotion, as the workers dusted themselves off and Baxter yelled frantically at anybody who'd listen, I slipped away from my station and started after the cow, stripping off my armor, hard hat, and boots all the while. When I got outside the plant, I watched with giddiness as the wounded cow galloped down Highway 28, amidst honking and swerving cars. For a brief moment she'd escaped. We'd escaped. Fool's gold is worth plenty if you believe hard enough.

CHAPTER 9

When I got home, a man I didn't recognize was standing on my front porch. His red hair was plastered to one side. He had a cheap little mustache and a cheaper three-piece suit. He spoke in a voice as wispy as his mustache. "Are you Frankie Avicious?"

"I'm ashamed to admit I am."

"This is for you." And he stuck out a large manila envelope.

I grabbed it. "What the hell is this?"

"It's from your wife. It's a summons for divorce."

"Say what?"

"Your wife has started an action for divorce. It's stated in the summons. The fault grounds are adultery and cruel and unusual treatment. This too is stated in the summons. The relief sought includes spousal support and division of property. Once again, this is stated in the sum—"

"This some kind of a joke?"

He grinned and shook his head. "No, sir, no joke."

"Cruel and unusual, she says? The only thing that's been cruel and unusual in our marriage is when the bitch has tried cooking."

"Have a good day, sir. You have been served."

With that snide remark, the little redheaded punk spun around and made his way across my burnt yellow lawn toward his idling Pontiac Bonneville.

It wasn't supposed to happen this way. This was a complication I needed about as badly as a parasite in my urinary tract. Without Ruth, a dead father-in-law did me no good. She'd get a couple of high-powered lawyers. With my history of abuse and adultery, they'd shut me out for sure.

But I'd invested too much in this endeavor to end up with nothing. I may have been a drunk and a whoremonger, but I was no quitter. I knew what I needed to do. I needed to return to the scene of the crime. I needed to clean up the mess, hide the body. That'd buy me a little time...

Outside the sun was slowly fading, but it was still hotter than the devil in a cardigan sweater. I hopped into my car and blew on the steering wheel. Then I hit the engine and started driving, my stomach aching from too much booze and not enough food.

I half expected Dick's house to be surrounded by emergency vehicles and cordoned off by yellow police tape. It wasn't. Everything was quiet and normal. I drove up the hill and parked the car in the driveway. Then I stepped outside. There were no clouds, no breeze.

Nobody lived within five miles of Richard Richardson, but I was still cautious. Like a bird of prey I stood on the top of the hill and gazed across the horizon, twitching, making sure there were no witnesses. And although there were no signs of life, I couldn't get over that discomforting feeling that someone was hiding behind a creosote bush just watching and laughing and waiting. I was under a lot of pressure. My mind was rebelling.

I opened the door and entered the foyer with its barrel-vaulted ceilings and antique wood beams. Somewhere in the distance music was playing, but it was hard to make out, a little blurry. Christ, where was that music coming from? Probably an alarm clock in a bedroom somewhere. I walked through the house quietly, careful not to wake the dead. The house was in the exact chaotic way I'd left it. Books and clothes and papers and paintings scattered across the floor. And Richard Richardson lying in the living room, his arms and legs contorted grotesquely.

Without wasting time, I got to work on the body. Richard Richardson was no pipsqueak, I can tell you that much. He must have enjoyed a good meal now and then. Plus, rigor mortis had set in, making it even more awkward to move him. At first I tried power-lifting him over my shoulder. I nearly ruptured my uterus. The son-of-a-bitch came crashing to the floor. Then I got smart and dragged him by the legs. It took me twenty minutes at least to get him out the house and loaded into the trunk. I slammed the trunk shut and spit on the ground.

I returned to the house and started cleaning. The job was overwhelming. I couldn't remember where everything went. I did the best I could. A few paintings might have gone on the wrong walls. Papers were stuffed in random drawers and cabinets. Clothes were thrown in closets. Since I couldn't recall where they kept their booze—was there a liquor cabinet somewhere?—I quickly downed it and threw away the bottles. You can never be too careful. The house ended up in reasonable shape. Not perfect, mind you, but nothing out of the ordinary. If a maid or a friend entered the house, there would be no shrieks of dismay, no gasps of disbelief.

Exhausted, I sat in the kitchen and lit a cigarette. I

rested my head against my hand and closed my eyes. I imagined I was with Scarlett in New England among the maples, all chimney red and Halloween orange, the leaves crunching beneath our feet as we walked along the quiet avenues...

I never heard the front door open. I never heard the footsteps on the hardwood floor. But when I looked up, I came face-to-face with a one-armed Mexican.

"Who are you? Where is Dick Richardson?" A thick scar extended from below his right eyelid down to his nostril. He wore third-hand clothes, the right sleeve of his plaid cowboy shirt pinned against his chest.

I rose from the chair and stuck out my hand. He didn't shake it. "I'm Frankie Avicious," I said. "But you can just call me Mr. Avicious."

"Okay..."

"I'm the son-in-law."

He glared at me suspiciously. "He never mentioned no son-in-law."

"Forgetful bastard," I said. "You want a drink?"

"Don't drink."

"How about a Dr Pepper?"

"Where is Dick Richardson?" he asked again. "He's supposed to be here."

I crushed out my cigarette on the sole of my shoe. "He went on vacation," I said. "Someplace tropical. Lebanon, I think."

"I'm supposed to clean the house today," he said. "Every Friday I clean the house. He's always here."

"Doesn't trust you to be here alone, huh? Afraid you

and some friends might steal back the state of Arizona?"

"No, that's not—"

"Well listen, amigo, you're in luck. I already cleaned the house. Top to bottom."

"You cleaned it?"

"I'm a bit of a neat freak, I must admit. I came over to borrow a book from Dad, Tony Robbins's classic *Awaken the Giant Within*, and I happened to notice some dust collecting in the corner of the butler's pantry. So I got down on my hands and knees and licked the marble floors clean. But while I was down there, I looked up and noticed some caviar caked on to the bottom of the cherry-wood shelves. And not the good stuff either. I think it was sevruga- or ossetra-style. Well, as you might imagine, one discovery led to another, and before I knew it, the whole house was as clean as a gibbon's ass. They spend a lot of time licking, you know."

The crippled Mexican took a step forward and squinted. "You sure you're related to him? You don't look the part."

"Yes, sir," I said. "Quite sure. But tell me something. You forget to bring your right arm with you this morning?"

He looked down, confirming that his arm was missing. Then he shook his head grimly. "No, mister," he said. "Work accident."

"You a gynecologist?"

"A what?"

"Where do you work?"

"Worked. No longer. Sunshine Foods."

"No shit?"

"No shit."

I stood at attention and saluted him. "Sunshine Foods,

making a better world, one cow at a time," I said.

"You worked there too?" he said, a smile appearing on his face.

I nodded. "Only reason I quit was due to some nagging psychological problems. Hebephrenia, the doctors called it. Yes, sir, my stint at Sunshine Foods was the most rewarding time of my life. Well, except for the time I was shipped to the Ivory Coast and sold as a slave on a cocoa farm. That was good fun too."

"It don't make no sense," the Mexican said. "If you're Mr. Richardson's son-in-law—"

"Then why didn't he get me a higher-paying, lower-risk job? You should ask him that sometime. I'm curious about that too. But tell me about your arm. Beef shredder? Rendering machine? Chain saw?"

"I stabbed myself," he said.

"Yeah?"

"I was a sticker—"

"Goddamn! You must be my brother from a different mother!"

"And on this day, the knocker was having trouble stunning the cattle. This one steer came to me really mad, trying like hell to break out of the shackles. I let the cow pass, figured I'd get it after it wore itself out a bit. I went to stick the next steer, turned my back, and the first one got in a good kick that caught me by surprise. Got me right in the arm. Being the damn fool I am, I didn't drop the knife, and I stuck myself right in the hand. Felt like I'd just stabbed another steer. For a few moments I didn't feel any pain. Then I looked at my glove and saw it was bright red, and I knew right away it sure as hell wasn't cow's blood."

As the Mexican blasted through his tale of woe, I felt a droplet of empathy running through my veins. The plant was full of kids like him who had been recruited out of Mexico with promises of milk and honey. The parent company, Cooper Ag, ran an office in Mexico City and advertised jobs to impoverished Mexicans. They even offered bus service to get the workers across the border, figuring they would be more likely to put up with the working conditions and low wages. Poor son-of-a-bitch.

"I came back the very next day," the Mexican continued. "You really only need one hand to stick. They put my name in the company newsletter. Second page. I've got it right here in my pocket. I always carry it around. They misspelled my last name…"

He handed me a folded piece of paper stained with coffee and hot sauce. I unfolded it. I'd never actually read one of the monthly newsletters, only used it on occasion to wipe my ass. It read: *"Give up after an injury? Not José Gutierrez. José has learned how to overcome the difficulties of working in a packing plant and is teaching others to do the same. Thanks, José, and keep up the fantastic work!"*

Poor son-of-a-bitch.

"But then my hand got infected. I would have gone to the doctor but—"

"No health insurance."

"I didn't have my citizenship papers in order. By the time I did finally get it checked out, it was too late. They cut it off. There are worse things that can happen to a man, you know."

He wasn't lying.

"You must despise my father-in-law," I said.

"Despise him? What are you talking about?"

The words rushed out of my voice box, only they weren't my words, they were the salesman's words. "He's made his fortune off the backs of working people like you. He chews you up and spits you out. All so he can live in his mansion and eat his caviar, and drive his fancy car. He was…he is a man of questionable character."

José shook his head and frowned. "No, no, you've got it all wrong. I don't have no problem with Mr. Richardson. He gave me a job when I didn't have one. He didn't hold a gun to my head. I knew the risks from day one. The choice was mine."

I laughed. "The hell it was. He manipulated you."

"After I got hurt, he could have kicked me to the curb. But he didn't. He gave me a job cleaning his house."

"For competitive wages, I'm sure."

A sneer spread across the Mexican's face, and he took a step forward so that his chest was inches away from mine. I could smell his breath, a mixture of pinto beans, carnitas, and cerveza. "You know what your problem is, amigo?" he said.

"Well, I've got hemorrhoids for one thing. And my hairline is receding. And—"

"You're not thankful. You don't appreciate the things you got. You're always complaining about the things you don't got."

"It's the American way, señor," I said.

The sneer remained on his face. "I'm gonna get to work now, Mr. Avicious."

"But I already told you. The house is clean."

"Then it'll be extra clean this week. That's not such a bad thing, is it?"

José started in the main floor bathroom, scrubbing and spraying, whistling happily all the while. Me, I sat back down at the kitchen table and lit a cigarette and started thinking and thinking. I thought about how morality is a strange game. Take murder, for instance. A fellow gets in a dispute with his neighbor. Maybe his neighbor stole something from him. Maybe he raped his wife. In any case, this fellow decides the only thing he can do is end his neighbor's life. So he goes to a pawnshop and buys a 9mm. The next day, he knocks on the door, and when his neighbor opens up, he guns him down, six shots in the chest. They send detectives and forensic investigators to find the poor son-of-a-bitch. Then they send in the lawyers and judges. When everything is said and done, he'll face a charge of first-degree murder and will likely be sentenced to life in prison or, perhaps, death. Meanwhile, our country gets in a dispute with another country. Maybe our enemy stole something from us, maybe they raped our women. We decide to go to war. We send our soldiers in fighter planes and tanks and tell them to kill, kill, kill. And if they do, if they succeed in killing our neighbors, do we charge them with a crime? No. We give them parades. We call them heroes.

I was no hero. But I was no monster either.

I knew what I needed to do about José Gutierrez, and it broke my goddamn heart in two. He was just in the wrong place at the wrong time. As soon as the Dick's body was discovered, he might go to the police, mention who he saw smoking cigarettes inside their kitchen. Yes, I knew what I needed to do.

He finished the bathroom and moved to the parlor. I walked slowly toward him, my weapon dangling from my hand. I cocked the gun and pointed it at him. He didn't seem surprised. He rose to his feet. "I have a family, señor. My daughter. She's going to be getting married next month."

"I'm sorry," I said. "Goddamn it, I'm sorry." Then I shot him three times. The first bullet knocked him to the ground. The next two ensured he stayed there.

I loaded José Gutierrez in the trunk, right on top of his benefactor. Then I drove slowly toward town. I got in my car and drove. I turned on the radio. It was filled with Gospel lies. "And Jesus said, 'Blessed are the poor in spirit: for theirs is the kingdom of heaven. Blessed are they that mourn: for they shall be comforted. Blessed are the meek: for they shall inherit the earth. Blessed are they which do hunger and thirst after righteousness: for they shall be filled. Blessed are the merciful: for they shall obtain mercy. Blessed are the poor in heart: for they shall see God.' And are you pure in heart? Have you washed the sins from your hands? Will you be spending eternity with the Savior, drinking the nectar of truth, or will you be burning with the devil in his fiery incinerator?" I turned off the radio.

I arrived at my house. I parked in the driveway and pulled out my final cigarette, a bent one with no life insurance policy. I reclined my seat and lit the cigarette. My wife had left me and there were two stiffs in the trunk of my car. Things can always get worse...

CHAPTER 10

I stored the bodies in the basement. It was a temporary solution, of course, just until I could use my considerable charm and good looks to win back my wife. In the meantime, there would be no bodies discovered, no murder investigation, no suspicions from Ruth about my ulterior motives. My window of opportunity was limited, I realized, because despite my good intentions, it wouldn't be long until the flesh started rotting and I had to move them once again. But for the time being, they were safe there, stuffed in sleeping bags filled with ice, buried beneath a mountain of back issues of *Penthouse* magazines. And for a couple of days, anyway, they were good and quiet.

Did I mention that Richard Richardson was divorced? Marilyn Cook was a martini-guzzling dildo-loving whore who could have benefited from a couple of hard slaps to her makeup-plastered face. At one time she'd been a nice addition to the Richardson fortune, a trophy wife with all the fixings. But time had sandblasted her face, and all the plastic surgery in the world couldn't salvage it. Dick had filed for divorce, reluctantly agreeing to pay a small monthly allowance. Marilyn had moved on with her life, getting remarried to a mailman who'd completed serving a six-month sentence for mail fraud, and buying a cat named Fluffy that suffered from a terrible case of psoriasis. Marilyn also maintained a loving relationship with her daughter. I figured she might know where Ruth was hiding.

The next day, I drove down to Main Street and got a haircut and a shave at Curl Up and Dye Barbershop. Then I went to the Clothes Line and bought a fresh pair of black jeans and a red-and-white-checkered cowboy shirt. Finally, I stopped at The Rehab Lounge to quench my thirst. After downing a few vodka and vodkas, I hopped into my car. I pissed on the steering wheel to cool it off and headed out toward Marilyn's place.

Her house was a two-bedroom ranch with RV parking, a trio of thirsty palm trees, and a spectacular view of the landfill. When Marilyn saw me, she made a surprised/happy expression and opened the door. Her face was stretched around her head a few times, and she was wearing more makeup than a prostitute clown. Her pink jogging suit revealed a wrinkled and sunburned bosom. Her badly dyed red hair was styled in a 1950s beehive. She was wearing a perfume that smelled an awful lot like Beefeater gin.

"Frankie, dear," she slurred, her painted eyebrows rising in arches. "So nice of you to stop by."

I nodded my head and stuck a grin on my face. "You're looking beautiful as ever, ma'am," I said. "Did you have some more cosmetic work done?"

She giggled. "You sweet boy. Flattery will get you everywhere. Please come in. I was just fixing a martini. I'll make two. And what would you like to drink?"

"A beer would be good."

I entered and sat down on the couch while Marilyn disappeared into the kitchen. She returned a moment later with a pair of martinis and a Pabst Blue Ribbon. I grabbed the beer and dumped it down my throat. I felt better. Marilyn sat down next to me, rubbing her long, plastic fingernails against her thigh. "I'm glad you stopped by," she whispered. "I get so lonely sometimes."

I shifted in my seat. "Yeah, well. I'm sure you have friends you could call."

"Oh yes. Many, many friends. But none of them are as strong and handsome as you." She licked her hooker-red lips and winked. At that moment, I heard some faint footsteps from down the hallway. I looked up and saw the silhouette of a man, but he quickly disappeared. Marilyn must have seen him too, because she rose to her feet and shouted in a shrill voice, "Fred. Get over here. We've got a guest, and you're being rude."

A few moments later, Fred appeared, his shoulders slumped and his head down. He was tall—he must have been six foot one—and thin, and he had a long, sad face. His brown hair was combed straight down over his forehead. I stood up and grabbed his hand. His grip was flimsy, and he allowed me to do all the shaking. "Good to see you again, sir," I said. "I just wanted to talk to your wife for a moment, and then I'll be on my way."

"Did you hear that, Fred?" Marilyn said. "Frankie wants to talk to me."

He sighed and nodded his head warily.

"Sit, Fred. You're making us all uncomfortable."

For a brief moment he glared at his wife, and I saw an overwhelming rage burning in his eyes. But the expression quickly changed to resignation as he moped over to the couch and sat down next to me. "So tell me, Frankie," Marilyn said. "Are you here for business or pleasure?"

"Well, actually it's about Ruth."

"Then it's certainly not pleasure. I can't believe you married that behemoth bitch. And I say that with the utmost love for my daughter. She called me, you know."

"Yeah?"

"Yes. She said you two had gotten into a terrible fight. She said you had become violent with her."

I shrugged my shoulders and grinned. "We had a misunderstanding," I said. "I gave her a little love tap."

Marilyn threw back her head and cackled. "A love tap, huh? Did you hear that, Fred?" He shrugged and sighed. "That's priceless, Frankie, absolutely priceless."

"I didn't expect you to believe me, ma'am. But it doesn't really matter, I suppose, since you don't seem to be all that concerned about your daughter's well-being."

Marilyn placed her right hand on her chest and fluttered her heavily painted eyes. "That's not fair," she said, frowning. "I love my daughter very much. You know that. But I also know she can have a bad attitude at times, and I know it's your responsibility to fix that bad attitude."

"My responsibility?"

"Yes, Frankie. Your responsibility. Do you read the Bible? Probably not. If you did, you would know a wife is the husband's property."

"Yeah? How about that? And I thought my television was the only thing I owned."

"And if she's giving you lip, if she's disrespecting your manhood, then it is your duty to act with authority."

"So what you're saying is I did the right thing."

"Absolutely, Frankie. You had to show her your might. You had to show her the man is the king of the castle. Unless, of course, you live with someone like my Freddy. He's pathetic, isn't he? A mailman. I married a mailman."

"Postal carrier," Fred said quietly.

"What?"

"Postal carrier," he said again.

"Oh, right," Marilyn said, rolling her eyes. "Excuse me. Postal carrier. There. Do you feel better, honey?"

Fred Cook didn't answer; he just rose from his seat and walked toward the hallway.

"And where do you think you're going?" Marilyn said.

"I'm going to the bathroom."

"Well. Fine. Just don't forget to sit down when you tinkle. I've got enough to worry about without having to clean up after you." He nodded his head and closed the bathroom door. Marilyn clicked her tongue a few times and furrowed her brow. "I swear, it's like living with an eight-year-old sometimes. If I allow him to pee standing up, he gets it all over the rim. Men can be so barbaric sometimes."

She took a long swallow of her second martini. "Anyway, Frankie, don't you worry. She might be gone right now, but she'll be back, mark my words. We women always come crawling back eventually. You just have to be patient."

I pulled out a cigarette and lit it. I looked around for an ashtray. Marilyn grabbed one out from the coffee table drawer and stuck it in front of me. "Patience," I said, "isn't something I can afford right now. I need to see her. Soon."

"Well, well, well. You're quite the eager beaver, aren't you?"

I grunted and sucked down some smoke. "Do you know where my wife is, or am I wasting my time?" I said.

"Of course I do."

"Okay then——"

"But first tell me why you're so desperate to see her."

"Well, Christ, she's my wife and I love her so I——"

Marilyn laughed falsetto-style and slapped her cellulite-filled legs. "Please, Frankie. Save your crap for the outhouse. I know you far too well."

I grinned. "Yeah, well, I guess you do. The truth is I have a monetary interest."

"Oh, I understand," Marilyn said, caressing my biceps. "You're worried you might miss out on her daddy's money-woney."

"It's a concern."

She sucked down the rest of her drink. What didn't fit in her slut mouth dribbled down her slut chin. "Well, don't worry, darling. Mama's here to help you. I'll tell you where Ruth's hiding." She leaned over and licked my cheek with her gin-marinated tongue. "But first you need to pay the toll."

"I think your husband might have some objections."

She laughed cruelly. "Fred is pathetic and weak. Besides, he gets off on watching other men violate his wife. He's a pervert."

So I was up Shit Creek without a paddle or a plunger. Marilyn Cook wasn't going to let me off easy, and I knew it. She rose from the couch, un-wedged her panties from her ass, and started performing some sort of ridiculous exotic dance. I covered my eyes, but she pried my fingers away from my face and continued with her torture session. Holding back the bile making its way up my throat, I watched as she slowly removed her top and revealed her saggy, wrinkled bosom. Then, giggling like a schoolgirl, she covered herself with her arms and raced into the bedroom. Resigned to my doom, I waited a few moments before following after her. When I opened the door, the only thing she was wearing was a creepy smile. Some top-forty music was playing on the stereo. She was lying in the canopy bed, her boobs hanging by her feet, and her legs shaking to the beat. "I know where your wife is," she said. "Make me feel good, Frankie, and I'll tell you."

Then she lay down on her stomach, turned her head around and purred. "I've been a bad girl, Frankie, such a bad girl. I think I deserve a spanking, don't you?"

I just stood in the doorway and shook my head.

"Oh, c'mon Frankie, don't humiliate me. Remember, I am your mother-in-law. Now come on over here and spank me."

It was a game I couldn't win. I walked over to the bed, placed one knee on the mattress, and slapped her bum gently and gentlemanly. "No, no, no," she said. "That's all wrong. You don't understand how bad I've been. Smack me. Smack me like the whore I am."

So that's what I did. It took a couple of minutes to get warmed up, but eventually I got going pretty good, just whaling on her big ol' booty until it turned red and swollen. She was breathing heavier and heavier, and I knew she was getting close, so I kept on going. Finally she came, and I swear to God I heard all the champagne glasses in the kitchen shatter. She rolled over and grinned, still panting like a pit bull in heat. "See?" she whispered. "I knew you could do it."

"Yeah," I said, blowing on my hands. "I met my end of the bargain, now you need to meet yours."

"Of course, darling. I would never go back on my word. Only—"

"Only what?"

"Is there any way you could slap me around just one more time? I haven't come like that since the Carter administration."

I shook my head. "Where's Ruth?"

"Oh, darn. But you can't blame me for trying, can you?" She grabbed her red panties from underneath the bed and put them on, covering her welt-covered ass. "She's staying with Simon Harris."

"Never heard of him."

Mrs. Cook laughed. "Well, you should have. After all, he almost married your wife."

Oh, that Simon Harris. Now I remembered. The two of them had been engaged when we first met. Ruth couldn't have picked a worse protector. Simon resembled a Muppet with anorexia. He couldn't have defended her from a hospice patient, much less a big bad wolf like me.

"Where does he live?" I growled.

"In Johnstown." She grabbed a piece of paper off the nightstand and wrote down the address. I snatched it from her hand.

"Have a good day, Mrs. Cook," I said. "If you have a chance, you might want to put some ice on that rump of yours."

She puckered her lips. "Oh, no. I want to savor each and every bruise you inflicted on me, you great brute."

On the way out of the house, I ran into Fred. He motioned for me to come near, and I did. He leaned in real close, giggled, and whispered in my ear. "When my wife passes on, I'm gonna piss on her corpse."

I nodded solemnly. "Don't blame you, Freddy," I said. "Don't blame you one bit."

CHAPTER 11

Johnstown, Arizona, was a town firmly entrenched in the new west, filled with shopping malls, chain stores, and fast-food restaurants that seemed to repeat every few blocks. The saguaros and prickly pines of the desert had been replaced by huge subdivisions with mass-produced homes.

Cars and trucks zoomed down Shields Boulevard, Johnstown's major artery. I drove slowly, keeping my eyes open for Lynn Street. When I found it, I hooked a right and drove past streets with names like Sunbird Drive, Falcon Court, and Soaring Eagle Way. Finally, I arrived at Simon's house. It was a contemporary two-story with a wood deck out front and a covered sandstone patio off to the side. The neatly trimmed lawn was lush green. I parked my car, checked my bad looks in the rearview mirror, and stepped outside. I opened up the gate on the white-picket fence and started toward the front door.

Simon answered before I had finished knocking. The scrawny son-of-a-bitch had grown a crooked blond mustache that looked as if it'd been pasted on his upper lip. His face was blotchy and covered with pimples. His chapped lips were spread into a frown. "What the heck are you doing here?" he whined. "You ain't welcome here."

"You've got something that belongs to me."

"Finders keepers, Avicious. Now get the heck off of my property, before I call the proper authorities."

I grinned sheepishly. "Oh, come on now, Simon. I just want to talk to her. I just want to set the record straight, tell her how much I love her, tell her how sorry I am."

But Sissy Simon wouldn't budge. "You've got some nerve coming around here," he said. "Especially after all the pain and sadness you've caused her. She's a special girl, and she doesn't deserve any of this heartache."

I nodded my head. "I couldn't agree with you more, Simon, and that's the God honest truth. So I guess I'll be heading out then. But before I go, there are a few things I want to tell you."

"Yeah?"

I was about to tell him how much I appreciated all he was doing for Ruth, how much I admired him for looking out for her when her husband was obviously such a monster, how I hoped I could someday repay him for all the trouble he'd gone through. Yeah, I was about to tell him all that, but at the last second I changed my mind. With a quick jerk of my head, I speared him in the temple. He staggered backward. Before he could react, I gave him a couple of jabs to the kidneys. He crumpled to the ground. I stepped over his body and made my way into the living room, which was decorated in a tasteful southwestern style, complete with plastic cactus wall hangings, coyote figurines, and Navajo rugs.

Ruth appeared from the bathroom, wearing only the king-sized comforter she used as a towel. When she saw me—and her poor battered Simon—she covered her mouth with her hands and backed up a few steps.

"Ruth," I said. "I just came here to set the record straight. I don't want to start any trouble. I just want to talk to you."

"Fuck you, Frankie," she said. "You're nothing but a beast, and beasts need to live in cages."

"I know you're angry, baby, and you've got every right to be. But you've got to listen to me, just for a minute. Let me say my peace, and then I'll leave. Promise."

She folded her arms and shook her head. "There's nothing you can say. We're through, and I mean it this time. I'm going to marry Simon like I should have done in the first place."

"You go on believing that, Sugar. But seriously, I've been doing a lot of thinking. Turns out, I was wrong. I never should've smashed you up the way I did. I don't know what got into me. Also turns out that I love you. Do you hear me? I love you. I love you more than a baby loves his mama's tit."

That's when I noticed that Simon had vanished. I'd had my back turned to him, and he'd managed to sneak past me into the bedroom. When he reappeared, his face was bright red and his jaw was clenched. In his right hand, he gripped a croquet mallet. I grinned. "Take it easy, Simon," I said. "Let's not do anything rash."

"I don't want you in my house," he said. "So go on and get out."

I took a quick step toward him and extended my arm. I was going to gently remove the weapon from his hand so nobody would get hurt. See, I knew a thing or two about croquet mallets and the irrevocable damage they could cause. But my sudden movement must have startled Simon. He lurched forward and swung wildly. I tried blocking the mallet with my arm but missed completely. It glanced off the side of my face, and I cartwheeled sideways into a crumpled heap on the freshly vacuumed floor.

Moments later, Simon—crazed by rage—dropped his mallet and pounced on top of me. He fought hard, and he fought dirty. He bit and scratched and slapped. He pulled my hair and pinched my skin and squeezed my balls. I didn't fight back, didn't see a reason to. The more sympathy I could garner from Ruth, the better my future standing would be. So, I remained lying flat on my back, offering no resistance, allowing this Muppet of a man to beat me into a bloody pulp.

Eventually, Simon's fury dissipated, and his body relaxed. He rose unsteadily, his jaw still clenched. I rolled over to my stomach and groaned. I thought my ribs might be broken. I pushed myself up to all fours, then willed myself to my feet. I wiped the blood from my face, grinning through the pain. Ruth cowered in the corner, covering her mouth with her hands, too shocked to say anything. And Simon, realizing the physical damage he'd leveled on me, closed his eyes, shook his head, and sobbed.

I stared straight into Ruth's moon face. "Come back to me," I said.

She took a step forward but then stopped. Without another word, I staggered out of the house, my woozy shadow in close pursuit.

After all that, I made a pit stop at The Mother Road Diner, a greasy spoon devoted to Route 66 and the American West. The décor was full of 1950s tackiness: old license plates, Burma Shave signs, Coca-Cola advertisements, and posters of muscle cars. The big-boned waitress with a coffeepot welded to her hand played her part too well, chomping on gum and calling everybody "Honey," and "Sugar."

I sat down in a booth, and she poured me some coffee. Bobby Darin was singing about sharp teeth. I pulled out a mangled cigarette from my pack and lit it. The waitress returned and asked if I needed any more time. I shook my head and ordered a slice of cherry pie and a slice of apple pie. And a slice of pecan pie because I was hungry. She wrote down the order and winked at me. "Looks like we might get some rain," she said. I looked out the window. Long streaks of metal-fence-post gray were appearing in the early evening sky, and the wind was kicking up dust.

I smoked my cigarette to the filter and drank my coffee to the grinds. I thought about hell. I heard it was pretty this time of year. My pies arrived. I devoured them, then used my napkin as a shroud. Feeling satiated, I rested my head in my hand and stared out the window.

And that's when I saw them. They were standing behind the streetlight, hidden by the shadows and the mist, but I could see them just fine. She was wearing a little blue dress and carrying a small red purse. Her bleach-blonde hair was slopped up in a greasy ponytail. He looked just like he always did: seersucker suit, porkpie hat. He was squeezing her hand and whispering in her ear. She was nodding and giggling.

I crushed out my cigarette and pulled my wallet out of my pocket. I dropped a ten-dollar bill on the table. Then I limped outside, my soul hanging on to my leg for dear life. The waitress said, "Y'all come back, y'hear?"

When I got outside, Scarlett was hurrying down the

avenue, her back toward me. But Marteau was gone. I'd seen him with my own eyes. Now he'd vanished. He was a vampire.

I walked briskly, then started jogging. I caught her at the corner. I grabbed her by the shoulder and spun her around. Her face was flush and she was out of breath. "Frankie," she said. "What are you doing here?"

"I saw you from the diner," I said. "I saw you talking to him."

She looked up and smiled, but her eyes were glazed over. "Saw me talking to who?"

"Jack Marteau."

"No. I don't know what you're talking about. I don't know any Jack Marteau."

"Jesus Christ," I said. "Don't treat me like a fool. I saw him with my own eyes. You were standing next to him in the shadows, talking, and then he fled. I couldn't see his face, but I saw his hat, his briefcase…"

"Poor Frankie," she said. "You've got it all wrong."

I shook my head and cursed. "I'm not crazy," I said. "I know what I saw."

Scarlett moved closer, causing me to choke on the dread filling inside my lungs. "You told me you were going to take me away," she said, touching my face with her knobby fingers. "But I've been waiting, waiting, waiting."

I grunted and spit on the ground. "I meant what I said."

"Did you? When then?"

"It won't be long now."

"That's good, Frankie. After all, what's the rush? We don't have to leave tonight. Tonight we could go to your place, and you could take me for a test drive. Would you like that, Frankie?"

I swallowed hard. "My wife might be returning…"

She laughed derisively. "For such a dull boy, you do an awful lot of talking."

"Not all talk," I said. "My car's parked across the street. I'll drive."

We got into my Beretta and I steered down the avenue. Feeling a bit shaky, I made a pit stop at the drive-through window of Pussy Liquors and bought a fresh bottle of gin. The bony old lady couldn't stop coughing as she handed me my change. I opened the bottle and took a long swallow. It tasted like formaldehyde. I drank some more. I handed the bottle to Scarlett. She took a healthy gulp. Then her eyes rolled back into her head and she laughed.

We arrived at my house. There were two corpses in the basement. I didn't tell Scarlett. Figured it might ruin the mood. We went to the bedroom. She sat down on the edge of the bed. She kicked off her boots and crossed her legs. I leaned against the wall. I took another swig of gin and wiped my mouth with my forearm. Without shame, she pulled her shirt over her head and laughed cruelly. Her breasts looked like bowling balls. Except they weren't as round or as black. And they didn't have holes in them. Her nipples were the size of half-dollars. Below her left tit was a purplish welt. Ponso had probably given her that. Or maybe Marteau. "Well?" she said.

"Looks good."

"And are you just gonna stand there?" she said.

I shrugged my shoulders. "Mind if I turn out the light? I like it better in the dark. More romantic."

"You do whatever you want, honey," she said. "I want

it to be special, the best time of your life."

I hit the light switch. It took a few moments for my eyes to adjust. I walked over to the bed and sat down. Scarlett leaned over and kissed my cheek. She smelled like sex. My body tensed. The anxiety was pounding within my chest cavity.

"There's nothing to be afraid of," she said...

"There's nothing to be afraid of."

"It's not right," I say. "We both know it's not right."

And she touches my cheek with the back of her hand. "You've got such pretty brown eyes," she says. "No wonder you drive the girls crazy."

"Daddy finds out, he's bound to...to—"

But she doesn't listen. She pulls me close, kisses my lips. My soul begins to rise...

And then Scarlett was gasping for air. My hand was around her throat, squeezing, squeezing. Her face was turning purple. I could've killed her. I didn't. I released my grip and let her catch her breath. Then I took it away again, grabbing a hold of her arm and twisting it behind her back. She didn't fight back, didn't tell me to stop. Some girls like it rough. With my free hand, I gave her a nice shove, slamming her against the mattress. Her head snapped back, and a squeal escaped from her mouth. I told her to be a good girl and lie on her stomach. She did as she was told. Then with my trembling hands I pulled the miniskirt down so her round ass was visible. She was coughing and having a tough time breathing. I didn't care. Whores have no souls. I licked her lower back. Then I bit her. She screamed, and I noticed my anxiety was gone. It had transformed into something else.

She told me she wanted it, she wanted it more than anything in the whole wide world. Or maybe she begged me to stop, to please, please stop. It didn't matter. With one quick motion I yanked down her panties so they were dangling from her ankle. I shoved my fingers inside her. I jammed them harder and harder until blood trickled down her thigh and she screamed in pain and I knew I was a monster oh Jesus save me.

I collapsed on top of her and we lay there in a heap of body parts, breathing heavily. Then Scarlett started crying. It took me by surprise. I tried comforting her by stroking her hair and telling her everything would be okay, but she kept on sobbing. After a while, I stopped trying to comfort her. I fell asleep. I dreamed I was dead.

When I woke up, I was still alive, and Scarlett was gone. I panicked. I rose to my feet. I put on my clothes. My mind was splintering. It was too late for me.

Voices were coming from the bathroom. Scarlett's voice. A man's voice. I knew who it was. He was feeding her lies. I mustered up some fury. I kicked open the door. Scarlett was standing in front of the mirror, brushing her long blonde hair. She was all alone. She was singing a song. I'd never heard it before. Maybe she'd made it up: "Don't you worry, little angel, let me chase away those fears. Mama's found herself a new love, and he's kissed away her tears." She had a lousy voice. It didn't bother me much. I walked across the bathroom and stood behind her, watching her reflection. She looked defeated. I felt a pang of regret, not for what I'd done (there is no free will), but for the possible consequences of my actions. I felt the urge, the compulsive need, to prove myself to her.

"My father-in-law. I killed him. Shot him dead." The voice came from my mouth, but it sounded like a stranger.

Cold. Ruthless.

Scarlett turned around and faced me, her eyes all puffy and bloodshot. "You shouldn't have done that," she said, but the words were halfhearted.

"I killed him for you," I said. "Don't you understand?"

A scornful grin spread on her face. "Sure I understand," she said. "How much does he have?"

"A lot."

"What about your wife?"

"I'll take care of her."

Another nasty grin. "So when are we leaving?"

"Soon."

And that's the way it was. Outside the wind began blowing, and I wished it would never stop, and all the dust and stink and misery would be swept right off this abandoned world to which I was chained.

CHAPTER 12

Later that night, Richard Richardson and José Gutierrez began rattling their bones. I was sitting in the living room, drinking whiskey from a straw and cheating at solitaire, when I heard a faint "thump, thump, thump" coming from the basement. I didn't pay it any attention. It was probably just a rat, I told myself, or perhaps a harmless burglar. I kept on drinking, covering my ears with clenched fists. But the thumping became louder and more distinct. Footsteps. Human footsteps. I became paralyzed with fear. I didn't know what to do. I turned on the television. A game show was on. A woman was jumping up and down, covering her mouth. She'd won a flatscreen TV. It was the greatest moment of her life. I finished my whiskey and grimaced. My liver was begging me to slow down. I went to the kitchen and vomited in the sink. I opened another bottle.

Soon the footsteps were echoing throughout the house. I thought about leaving, going to a bar. This was crazy. There was an explanation for all this. The furnace was rattling. That was it. Old houses can make some strange sounds, especially after you've drank too much.

I went into the bedroom and grabbed my sticking knife. A fellow can never be too careful. Outside a coyote howled. Or was that just my imagination too? I opened the basement door and fumbled for the light. As soon as the light flashed on, the echoing of footsteps stopped. I walked down the stairs, the boards creaking beneath my feet, the knife dangling from my hand. I stepped over piles of junk and forgotten treasures until I came to the bodies. They were still dead. Thank God for small favors. The Mexican looked pretty good, besides the holes in his chest. But Big Dick was in bad need of a mortician. His skin was turning green, and his eyes and tongue were protruding. The stink would be starting soon. There was no sense in worrying. I needed to get some sleep. I turned and started back toward the stairs. And that's when Dick Richardson spoke. "They're playing you for a fool," he said. I dropped the knife and it clattered to the floor. I turned around. Dick rolled to his side and winked at me. And the Mexican's lips spread into a mocking little grin.

I'd gone crazy before. Back when I was in prison, I went through a long period of violence and rage. They stuck me in solitary, but then I started hurting myself— banging my head against the wall and biting through my own lip. Eventually they sent me to the psych ward, which was a hell of a thing. They chained me spread-eagle to a bed and shot me with a drug called Prolixin. I don't know what the purpose of the drug was, but it turned me into a zombie. I spent three weeks sitting in the corner of the room just staring at the wall, unable to sleep or speak. I could hardly eat, and everything was a major effort—it took me a good fifteen minutes to stand up and take a piss. Then the hallucinations started. I got regular visits from my dead father, a childhood friend named Charlie, and a wicked priest from my past. Most of the day I spent with my hands covering my ears, trying to block out the horrifying things they were whispering to me.

That bout of insanity could be attributed to the dope they pumped through my veins. But this experience couldn't be so easily explained. I wasn't going crazy, or at least I didn't think I was…

I walked over to where Dick was resting comfortably and gave him a couple of quick jabs to the stomach. "Think you can scare me?" I said. "The hell you can. I'm taking the two of you out back and burying the both of you. That'll teach you."

I started with the Mexican. He was slight, so it wasn't so difficult. I grabbed him around the torso, bent at the knees, and pulled him up the stairs. Then I propped him against the wall. He asked for a cerveza. I spit in his face. Then I went back downstairs. Moving Big Dick Richardson was a different story. It was akin to a malnourished Ethiopian boy pushing a truck up a snow-packed hill. Or the Virgin Mary delivering triplets. But I was plenty motivated. I worked hard and I worked fast. By the time I'd got him up the stairs, I was sweating like an obese Eskimo in an overcrowded sauna. I was as tired as a one-legged dwarf after running the Boston Marathon. I sat him next to the Mexican. Then I slumped down next to them. I removed my shirt and glared at Dick. He winked at me. He was trying to get under my skin. He was succeeding.

I closed my eyes and tried to calm my mind. When I reopened them, Richard Richardson had moved a couple of inches closer to me. And José Gutierrez was giggling. With rage and panic crawling on my skin, I pulled my head back and speared the Mexican in the temple. He gasped, barely audibly. Then I leapt to my feet and started on Big Dick. I kicked and stomped and punched and screamed. By the time I was through with him, his shirt was torn, his arm was broken, and his face didn't look much like a face anymore. I spit on the ground and forced a chuckle through my windpipe. And that's when I heard someone pounding on the door...

Ponso Arguello's gravelly voice echoed through the empty halls, all infused with nastiness and fury. "I'm gonna kill you, motherfucker, I'm gonna kill the both of you!"

There was nothing I could do. I wasn't going to be able to talk my way out of this one. I shat and pissed my pants. I vomited all over myself. Then I grinned like a madman. A quarter century passed before Ponso entered. His face was as red as a used tampon. A vein was bulging from his neck. He was plenty mad and was ready to brawl. He knew that Scarlett, his God-given property, had been to my place, and now his imagination was getting the best of him. A jackknife was welded to the palm of his hand, and I'm damn near sure he meant to use it.

And then he saw the corpses.

At first he didn't react. He just stood there, eyes blinking, his brain not equipped to comprehend the carnage in front of him. Then the color drained from his face and all the macho rage dissolved into childlike fear. "What's this?" he said, as if somebody had just dropped a package in front of his house.

"I'm gonna have them stuffed," I said. "Stick them on the mantel or something."

Ponso backed up a few steps. He was scared. Maybe he'd never seen a dead man before. "I didn't really want to kill them," I said. "I just ain't the killing type. Not unless they deserve it."

Realization came slowly for Ponso, pausing at each neuron to make sure. He collapsed to his knees and grabbed his stomach. His hands turned red. "What the fuck?" he said. But his voice was trembling. They all act tough until it's time to play ball...

"You shouldn't have come here," I said. "You shouldn't have trespassed. There are laws against that. Now I've got every right, every right in the world to...to..."

Ponso lunged at me, but his heart wasn't in it. Fear had sapped him of his meanness. I sidestepped him and gave him a quick jab to the solar plexus. He doubled over, grunting and wheezing. The knife clattered to the floor. I kneed him in the chin, jerking his head upward. Then I shoved him against the wall and started pounding, all the years of fear and anger and hurt exploding from my muscle fibers, relentless, relentless, relentless.

After a while, Ponso stopped resisting, and his body went limp. He slumped to the floor a few feet from the corpses, his head propped up by the wall. He was still breathing, but there wasn't much life left.

I hovered over him for a few moments, hyperventilating. My head was spinning, and I was having a hard time focusing. The booze and bastards were taking their toll. I leaned against the wall and pulled out a cigarette. I tried lighting it, but my hands were shaking too much. I threw it on the ground. Ponso groaned and started stirring. I didn't move. He got on all fours and started crawling across the room. He was trying to reach for the knife. I stomped on his hand. He didn't scream, just dropped his head in dejection. I bent down and picked up the knife. I turned him over so he was lying on his back. He opened his eyes and looked into mine. I'd seen those eyes before.

In steers. No longer terrified. Just resigned. I'd done it a million times before. This time was no different. Slice that carotid artery. Drain him of his blood. When we're living and eating and buying, we're the kings of the world, masters of the universe. But when we're dying, we're just animals, fucking animals. I pressed the knife against his neck. Then I jammed it through. He gurgled and twitched. And he died. Just like an animal.

CHAPTER 13

Circumstances beyond my control. Three fucking corpses in my living room. One thing was certain. There was no escape for me this time. I paced through the empty hallways. They'd kill me. Lethal injection. Paralysis of respiratory muscles. Cardiac arrest. My last meal: Filet mignon. French fries. Cherry pie. To hell with it.

I crawled through the house: go cockroach, go! I picked up the phone. I knew his number by heart. I'd always known his number by heart.

He answered before the first ring. "I need to speak with you," I said.

"Yes, Frankie. I thought you might."

"Richard Richardson is dead," I said.

"Dead?"

"And rotting in the hallway."

"Oh dear. Messy."

"And these two other fellows. José Gutierrez. Ponso Arguello. They showed up at the wrong time. I had to kill 'em both."

"And you're calling me because—"

"I'm in a bind here, Jack. I figured you could help me."

He was quiet for a few moments. No, that's not right. He was talking to somebody else, covering the phone with the palm of his hand. Finally he spoke to me. "Tell me,

Frankie, how familiar are you with the ins and outs of Sunshine Rendering?"

"Familiar. I worked there for two years."

"Wonderful. Perhaps then you have heard about the recent spate of complaints filed against the plant. Air quality, workers' rights. Those sorts of things. The whole world is going crazy. But the short of it is that the city has forced the company to make some concessions. The plant is now only allowed to run its boilers for twenty hours a day. It closes at eleven, at which point the cleaning crew works for two additional hours. From one o'clock to three o'clock the plant is shut down and, other than a six-dollar-an-hour security guard, nobody is on the premises."

"What does that have to do with me?" I said. "What does that have to do with three stiffs?"

"Everything is falling into place, Frankie. The perfect setup is right there in front of your nose."

"What the fuck are you talking about?"

For the next hour or so, Marteau talked and I listened. He told me what I was going to do, he told me exactly what I was going to do. And I knew that hell wasn't too far of a drop.

Outside the sun was setting, and the sky looked like a bad watercolor painting, all smeared orange, red, pink, and purple. I went into the kitchen and grabbed myself a beer. It tasted like nun's piss. I drank four more. Then I returned to the hallway where my science project was picking up steam. Dick Richardson now officially stank. The others weren't far behind. My only saving grace was the fact that meatpacking towns always stink, and it was hard to distinguish one odor from another. But it wouldn't be long before the maggots found them. I didn't have much time. I needed to get busy.

I'd left Ponso's knife on the floor, right next to his corpse. Now, per my conversation with Marteau, I needed to use the knife again. Planning, planning, planning.

I don't know if you've ever tried cutting the finger off a human being, dead or alive, but assuming you have, you know it's not as easy as it might sound. Unless the knife is exceptionally sharp, it takes a little bit of effort, a little bit of sweat. With all those muscles and bones and ligaments stuffed inside the skin, it's a little like cutting a piece of steak with a butter knife. Thankfully, Ponso's blood had pooled in the lowermost vessels, and the operation was a fairly neat one. It felt strange to hold his detached finger in my hand, but I guess it didn't matter much to him.

Ponso's SUV was parked out front. It was a half-ton Chevy Suburban with plenty of cargo space. On the back window were two stickers: one pledging support for our troops, the other encouraging everyone to "Eat More Pussy" (which I certainly planned to do). In Ponso's hurry to skin and gut me, he'd left the car unlocked, keys in the ignition.

I'd wised up since my first experience moving a dead body. This time, armed with an industrial-sized wheel barrow I'd borrowed several months ago from the slaughterhouse, I was much better prepared. I loaded all three of them up into the SUV, one on top of the other. Then I went back into the house and drank some booze and sniffed some glue. Then I used a rusted nail to carve a tattoo onto my forearm. It said "Dead Man."

***

It wasn't wise, perhaps, to keep returning to the scene of the crime, but for the plan to be executed, it was necessary. Whistling a children's song, I drove to Dick's oversized shack and parked in the driveway. And while Ponso's detached finger and I went inside, I made sure to leave the windows to the car cracked. You hear about it all the time in the desert, people suffocating in hot cars, lack of breathable air and such. I wanted to make sure Dick, Ponso, and José were comfortable. It was the least I could do.

The way a house looks after a burglary is different from the way it looks after a simple assault. A burglarized house is typically torn apart, one drawer at a time. Valuables, ranging from jewelry to electronics, are missing, and papers and clothes are strewn across the floor. Meanwhile, there is usually nothing taken after a simple assault, and other than some busted furniture and lamps, the house is left in relatively decent shape. So I didn't want to get too crazy this time. I kicked open the front door. That was a good touch. I flipped over a few chairs and threw a Tiffany lamp on the floor. There was a disturbance here, an unwanted intruder. But who? They'd dust the place for prints. Might even find mine. That'd be okay. I was his son-in-law. Of more interest would be the numerous fingerprints of one Ponso Arguello. Forensic investigators didn't miss a thing nowadays. I pulled Ponso's finger out of my pocket and got to work.

After a while I glanced at my watch. It was past midnight. I needed to hustle. I hopscotched into the kitchen and pulled open the top drawer beneath the china cabinet.

Inside was a pair of brass keys. Just like Marteau had promised. I stuck them in my back pocket, a giggle escaping from my lips.

The security guard sat in a cage at the entrance of the parking lot. He was a skinny old black man gnawing on some beef jerky. In my most authoritative voice, I explained to him that I was Richard Richardson's son-in-law—you do know who Richard Richardson is, don't you—and that I needed to get inside to recover some important documents he'd left there. From the back of the SUV, Dick's corpse protested, "Don't listen to him! He's a liar, a deceiver! He's up to no good!"

Then Ponso piped up. "Son-of-a-bitch! Son-of-a-bitch!"

And José. *"Aye Dios mio! Aye Dios mio!"*

"I'm sorry, mister, but the plant is closed. You can come back during business hours."

I shook my head. "That's no good." I pulled out my ID card. "I myself work over at the Sunshine Foods. Upper management. My business here won't take long."

"Come back tomorrow," he said.

I cursed and pulled out my wallet. Then I took out a hundred-dollar bill. I flattened it out, placed it on the counter. "If you'd reconsider..."

The gate jerked open.

I drove around to the back of the plant and parked in the empty parking lot, hidden by the long shadows of the smokestacks. I stepped out of the SUV. I felt dizzy. I steadied myself by grabbing hold of the pavement. After resting for a few moments, I pushed myself back to my feet, licked the blood off my face, and opened up the side door of the SUV. I pulled out the wheelbarrow. Then I walked to the back and opened up the trunk. The bodies had shifted, and now they were all tangled up in each other. I struggled for a few minutes until I had them disengaged. Big Dick was about to make another wisecrack, so I punched him in the groin and said, "Aren't you tired of the pain?" I loaded Ponso and José into the wheelbarrow, leaving Dick to stew in the SUV.

The plant was built in 1932, and they hadn't done much updating. No keyless card entries. Just dead bolts. I pulled Dick's keys out of my pocket. The first two didn't work. I panicked. The third key did the trick. I farted with relief.

Like Sunshine Foods, the inside of the rendering plant was filled with steel catwalks, crisscrossing conveyer belts and white pipes. There was an Eisenhower-era utilitarian feel to it. But the stench here was overpowering, ten times worse than the slaughterhouse. Decaying flesh. All kinds. Cattle, hogs, sheep, raccoons, possums, snakes, cats, dogs. You name it, Sunshine rendered it.

I walked slowly through the plant, pushing the wheelbarrow, zigzagging through the machinery and carcasses. Eventually I came to what the workers affectionately called the "Blood Hole," a ten-foot-deep stainless steel pit loaded with a giant auger-grinder. It was used to chop and grind the flesh, prepare it for cooking.

One after another, I pulled the corpses out of the wheelbarrow, dragged them across the concrete, and shoved them into the Blood Hole. Running my hand through my hair, I walked over to the far wall and opened up a plastic cover. I hit the switch. The auger started with a low roar. I sat down on a bench and opened a package of Twizzlers. I stuffed one in my mouth, closed my eyes, and listened to the grinding of the echo against the steel walls.

Eventually the grinding stopped. I waited a while and ate another Twizzler. Then I peered inside. They were gone. There were only chunks of their flesh. The workers wouldn't think twice. Like I said, you name it, Sunshine rendered it.

I left the plant and locked the doors behind me. I hopped back into Ponso's car. I drove down the highway a ways until I came to a little dirt pull-off next to a refinery tower. That's where I—that's where Ponso—ditched the car, with poor Richard Richardson's body stuffed in the back. It wouldn't take long for them to find Richard's body now. And the car, of course, would be traced back to a Mr. Ponso Arguello. They'd search for him for a while, but I was pretty confident they wouldn't find him. And as for José Gutierrez? Well, a missing Mexican immigrant isn't anything to get worked up about. They're called disposable workers for a reason. I stuck my hands in my pockets and started the long walk home.

The night was so dark and quiet and peaceful. I closed my eyes and suddenly felt his presence. My eyes welled up with tears. I dropped to my knees. To think he had sent his only son to bleed and die on that cross for a wretch like me. I was overcome with awe and gratitude. I didn't deserve it, I know I didn't deserve it. But I was going to make the most of it. I was going to go on killing and whoring and stealing and cheating, and there wasn't a goddamn thing he could do about it. All of my sins forever forgiven because of his never-ending love. Buyer beware…

CHAPTER 14

I guess even a hard-luck fellow like me was bound to run into some good fortune eventually. When I arrived home that morning, Ruth Avicious was in the kitchen standing in front of the stove, looking something like an obese June Cleever, cracking eggs into a frying pan. "Hi, sunshine," she said, smiling. "Can I pour you some coffee?"

"Yeah, yeah. Go ahead."

She dumped some mud into a mug and slid it in front of me. The coffee was so weak an armless boxer could've knocked it down. A few minutes later, Ruth handed me my breakfast: burnt toast, runny scrambled eggs, and a mystery meat. Normally I would have politely declined the slop Ruth had concocted, but I was hungrier than a fasting Ethiopian, so I quickly stuffed the food into my mouth and washed it down with a glass of spoiled whole milk. Ruth sat at the table and watched me eat, a sly smile glued to her face.

"So you had a change of heart?" I said.

"Maybe." Then she nodded her head and looked pensive, biting her fingernails. "There's something I've got to know, Frankie. I mean, before I recommit to you."

"What's that?"

"When you showed up at Simon's house, you said you loved me, you said I'd always be in your heart. Did you mean it?"

I belched and farted. Then I placed my hand on her thunder thigh. "I know I haven't always been the best husband," I said. "I drink and smoke too much, and maybe I've been a little rough with you sometimes. But I love you, Ruth Avicious, and I want our love to expand. Hell yes I do."

She brought both hands to her mouth, and her eyes quickly filled with saltwater. "Oh, Frankie," she said. Then she threw her arms around me and squeezed me tight. My shirt was quickly soaked with warm tears and snot. I hadn't seen her so happy since McDonald's introduced Super Sizes.

"Your boyfriend gave me quite a beating," I said. "With a croquet mallet, no less."

"Oh, your face doesn't look so bad," she said. "I mean, no worse than usual."

"There is just one other thing," I said. "The lawyer came by the other day with the divorce papers—"

"I'll call him first thing in the morning," she said. "The only thing that matters is we're together, and I love you and you love me and we live happily ever after together, just the two of us."

I almost burst out laughing. The thought of me being happy with my elephant turd of a wife was good for a chuckle if nothing else. But I managed to restrain myself. Instead of laughing, I smiled my most earnest smile and said, "And we will live happily ever after, darling. Just like Cinderella and her seven dwarfs."

"And seeing how we're so committed," Ruth said, "I was thinking that maybe we could spend some time together today. We could maybe take a walk in the park or a drive into the country. And then later on"—she walked her stubby fingers up my leg—"we could rent out a room at the Paradise Motel and have us some fun."

I picked up Ruth's hand and dropped it onto her lap. "Yeah, well that all sounds mighty tempting. Unfortunately, I've got a little business that needs attending to, so I'll have to take a rain check. Damn, and I've been craving a walk in the park."

Ruth studied me for a moment, trying to judge my sincerity, then shook her head and slammed her fist against the table. "Damn you, Frankie Avicious. You've always got an excuse at the ready. Maybe Simon is right. He warned me that you'd never change, that you'd always be a self-absorbed bastard."

I was about to tell her to shove it where she shits, but I caught myself. "Now, hold on just a second, sweetheart," I said. "You're not being fair. You know I want to spend time with you. I'll tell you what. Why don't I take care of my errands this afternoon, and then we can have a little romance tonight. We can order some pizza, maybe have a few Budweisers and then—"

The expression on her face softened. "Now you're talking," she said.

"Damn right I am." I licked my plate clean, stretched my body, and got to my feet. I was feeling pretty good about myself. I started toward the bathroom to empty my bowels when I heard Ruth's voice again. I stopped and turned around.

"I'm going to be thinking about you all day," she said.

"Likewise," I said, grinning.

"And Frankie?"

"Yeah?"

"If you don't fuck me tonight, then I'm leaving again,

and this time it'll be for good."

I nearly choked on the bile in my throat. "Fair enough, sweet tits," I said. "Fair enough."

I went to a pawnshop and bought a ring with the biggest fake diamond I could find. I wore it out on my pinkie. Then I went to a tattoo parlor and got Scarlett's name tattooed on my chest in Gothic font.

About three miles east of Huerfano proper stood an old abandoned amusement park called Fun City. The owners had skipped town years ago and left all their rides behind. The town of Huerfano was too cheap to do anything about it, and it had become a darkened carnival for drunks, runaways, and fuck buddies. Ms. Acres had agreed to meet me there.

I parked my car and stepped outside. The wind was complaining about something. I walked around for a while looking for some type of an entrance, but there wasn't one. Gritting my teeth, I clambered up over a barbed-wire fence, tearing my shirt and hands on the way down. I wandered through the grounds, past a broken-down Tilt-a-Whirl, a darkened house of mirrors, a horse-less carousel, and the skeleton tracks of a roller coaster. Finally, I came to the towering Ferris wheel where Scarlett was waiting. She was wearing jean shorts and a T-shirt that said "My Other Boyfriend's a Millionaire." I opened the latch and motioned for her to step in the gondola, then followed after her. I removed a cigarette from my shirt pocket and lit it.

"You could have come to my house," she said. "Ponso's not around."

I shook my head. "We can't be seen together. Not now."

"No?"

"I don't have time to explain. Do you trust me?"

"No."

"It doesn't matter. You've got to do something for me."

"I've done a lot for you."

"You need to call the cops. Tell them you're worried. You were having an affair. Your boyfriend, Ponso, found out. He went ballistic. Said he was going to kill your lover. And you haven't heard from either of them since."

Scarlett crossed her legs and leaned forward. She was wearing too much perfume. She always wore too much perfume. "That's quite a story," she said. "And who exactly was I having an affair with?"

"Richard Richardson."

There was silence for a few moments. "What are you doing, Frankie?"

"Ponso's dead," I said. "He tried to kill me. I killed him first."

Scarlett didn't bat a mascara-drenched eyelash. She didn't seem surprised or sad. "So you're setting up a dead man."

"He won't mind," I said.

Scarlett snorted. "You must trust me an awful lot. Telling me about all these people you've killed."

"And should I?"

"I'm not going to rat you out if that's what you're wondering. But what makes you think they'll believe me, a stripper?"

"They'll believe you because you are a stripper. You

make a living out of selling lies."

"Fuck you," she said. "You're not so noble yourself. Killing people and all that."

"I'm complimenting you, Sugar. We all lie. You just do it better than most. It's the perfect setup, Scarlett. I've taken care of the rest. There's a lot of money at stake."

"I'm crazy to believe in you," she said.

"Being crazy ain't so bad," I said. And without further ado, I unbuttoned my shirt and showed her the tattoo.

Her eyes opened wide. "What the hell is that?"

"Your name. Next to my heart."

She curled her upper lip and snorted. But I wasn't done. I pulled out the diamond ring. "So here's the deal. Figure I'll leave my wife one of these days. Figure we'll get married. You don't have to decide right now. Think it over. Scarlett Avicious. Got a nice ring to it, doesn't it?"

"Sure, Frankie, sure. Where's the box?"

"The box? What the fuck do you need the box for?"

"All expensive rings have boxes."

"I'll go to the dumpster. I'll find you a box."

A scornful grin spread on her face. I wanted to slap it away. Instead I kissed her, mashing my lips against hers, drawing blood. She pulled away. "My, my, you're a little on the rough side, aren't you?"

"Sorry."

"Don't apologize," she said. "I like it that way. Hubby."

I left Scarlett dangling in the Ferris wheel and returned to my car. Everything was falling into place. Someone was watching me from below. Now, if I could just endure my romantic evening with Ruth...

I didn't go home, not right away anyway. See, I started

thinking about Ruth's ultimatum—the one about knowing her in the biblical sense—and I couldn't bear to go
through with it. Don't get me wrong. I'd been with my
share of unsightly chicks. You know, girls that had fallen
off the ugly tree, hitting every branch on the way down.
But asking me to have relations with my wife? Frankly,
that was inhumane. So I went from bar to bar, liquor
store to liquor store, creating excuses for avoiding Mount
Ruth. There were the usual standbys: a headache, too
much stress at work, exhaustion. Then there were the
more creative alibis: I'd donated sperm earlier in the day,
I feared I'd caught herpes from myself, or I'd gone to
church that evening and didn't want to do anything to
soil my spirituality. But in my heart I knew my excuses
wouldn't work. I knew I'd have to face Ruth and her
love-blubber eventually. I knew that avoidance would
only cause more misery. I needed to go home. And I
would. After one more drink.

By the time I finally pulled into my driveway, the sun was
setting below the desert floor and the sky was filled with
blood from the dying day. I stepped outside. A couple of
kids came racing around the corner on their bikes, and I
cursed at them. I made my way across the burnt lawn.

I opened the front door. The lights were turned off and
a dozen or so candles were flickering. Some John Tesh
was playing—so very smooth!—and a path of dead rose
petals led to the bedroom. For a moment I considered
turning and running for my miserable life, but I quickly
changed my mind. I couldn't afford to have Ruth leave
me, not yet anyway. I needed to face my destiny.

I took a deep breath and stepped into the bedroom. The horror, oh the horror! Ruth was lying on the bed naked except for the potato sacks she called a bra. "Are you ready, big boy?" she purred.

I cleared my throat. "Well, actually, I was thinking I'd curl up with a nice book—*Bridges of Madison County* maybe—and then do a crossword."

"No, you don't, silly boy. Come sit next to Mama."

I stood there for a moment thinking about the agony I would soon be forced to endure. The buzz I'd accumulated over the course of the previous hours had all but disappeared, and I knew I wasn't going to survive tonight sober. No sense in being the hero. I pulled out the bottle of whiskey stuck in my boot and downed as much as I could as fast as I could. Then, like a Japanese kamikaze pilot, I readied myself for destruction. I dove into bed and was quickly smothered by the beached whale that was my wife.

She pulled down my pants. She tried yanking off my boxers. I shoved her away. I pretended I was somewhere else—the beach, next to a mountain stream, in the jungles of Vietnam—anywhere but in a bed with my head being crushed between Ruth's thunder thighs. I won't sicken you with the gruesome details. I will only say that the sex was hot and heavy with the emphasis on the heavy.

Finally, the battle ended. I crawled over the carnage—the arms, the legs, the tits—and stumbled into the bathroom. My stomach was rumbling. The slop I'd eaten for breakfast was ready to make a jailbreak. I sat down on the pot, my face covered in sweat. And that's when I heard someone knocking on the front door.

I poked my head out of the bathroom. Ruth was lying

on the bed smoking a cigarette, smiling like the canary that had swallowed the cat. "You expecting someone, Sugar-Butt?" I asked.

She shook her head. "No, it's probably our neighbor Mrs. Martin. I'll bet we woke her up with our debauchery."

Ruth managed to get out of the bed without tipping it over. She put on her bathrobe and disappeared into the living room. I sat back down on the toilet, remembered what I'd just done, and began hyperventilating. The front door opened, and I heard a man's voice, but I couldn't hear what was being said. Then I heard a loud scream and the sound of broken glass.

CHAPTER 15

Ruth was sitting on the floor, her legs folded beneath her Jupiter ass, her matted hair covering her face. She was moaning and her shoulders were rising up and down. Tears were spilling to the hardwood floor.

A man was standing over her, looking unaffected. He was a short pudgy guy with Charlie Brown–style hair, a boxer's nose, and a five o'clock shadow. His eyes were beady and suspicious—detective's eyes.

"What the hell's going on?" I said. "Who are you?"

He took a step forward, nodded solemnly. "Detective Don Johnson."

"Don Johnson? Weren't you on that *Miami Vice* show?"

"Different Don Johnson. Just talked to your wife…it's always hard. Her father was found dead late last night. Murdered."

I stared at the detective for a few moments, glassy-eyed. Then I shook my head slowly, a smile painted on my face like a clown who's been stabbed in the gut. "There must be some mistake," I said. "Why, I just spoke to him the other day—"

"There's no mistake, sir," Johnson said.

I flew through denial and dove right into the anger phase. "Who would have done such a thing?" I said with barely restrained fury. "What depraved maniac would have killed that fine person?"

Johnson smoothed back the fuzz on his scalp and shook his head. "We've got some leads," he said.

"Whoever did this will have to face the judgment of man and the wrath of God," I said.

Johnson eyed me warily. "I've got some questions. Shouldn't take long."

At this point, Ruth struggled to her knees and raised her arms up to hell, half screaming, half sobbing, "Why, why, why?" I walked across the room and kneeled next to her. Gingerly, I placed my arm around her and kissed her forehead, displaying to the detective obvious compassion and empathy in this early stage of mourning. Ruth shoved her face into my chest, the tears spilling down her cheeks and onto my shirt. I held my composure pretty well for a while, but then the overwhelming agony of the moment must have gotten to me. The next thing I knew, I too was crying, not subtle sniffling and sobbing, mind you, but unrestrained, full-out blubbering. And the strange thing about it is that the emotions felt genuine; the weeping was truly involuntary. I guess that hearing firsthand about such a senseless and brutal crime really struck a raw nerve. So the two of us just sat there in a heap, endless gobs of sorrow draining from our souls. Detective Johnson hovered over us, his hands clasped behind his back.

Several minutes later, Johnson repeated his request for interviews. We weren't suspects, mind you. The detective simply wanted to obtain as much information about the victim as possible. So as not to prejudice our answers, Johnson met with us separately, interviewing Ruth first while I lay in the bedroom reliving that fateful day's events and rehearsing my answers to anticipated questions.

Johnson met with Ruth for some time. Irrationally, I imagined they were talking about me, that Johnson was laying out his theory about how I, a convicted felon and a suspect in my own father's death, had butchered Dick Richardson to become a rich man. The paranoia growing, I plotted my escape. One thing was for certain, I wasn't going to let them lock me up in a cage again, no way, no how.

But when Johnson entered the bedroom, he didn't accuse me of anything. He blinked a few times, glanced around the room, and pulled out a half-smoked cigar. He patted his pockets for a few moments, searching for a lighter. I grabbed one off the nightstand and tossed it to him. He grunted a thanks. He lit the soggy cigar and puffed a few times, his eyes narrowing into slits. Then suddenly his mouth opened wide as if he were about to sing the national anthem. The color of his face changed from pasty white to red, saliva dribbled down his chin, and he started coughing uncontrollably. Frantically, he pulled an inhaler out of his pocket, stuck it in his mouth and breathed deeply, his eyes shut tight. After a couple minutes, his color returned, and the asthmatic episode was finished. His face relaxed, he stuck the inhaler back in his pocket, and returned the cigar to its rightful position between his lips. He patted down his forehead with a handkerchief and cleared the phlegm from his throat. "Sure do appreciate your time," he growled, as if nothing had happened.

I pointed to a wicker chair in the corner of the room. "Do you want to sit down? Can I get you some water?"

He shook his head. "I'll stand. Got a bad back. And I don't like water. No taste."

"Suit yourself," I said. I sat down on the edge of the bed and massaged my shoulders. The stress was really building, boy. I was as tight as an Amish schoolgirl.

"Gonna call you Frankie, if that's all right," he said.

"Call me whatever you want, just don't call me late for supper."

Johnson studied me for a moment before licking his fat fingers and flipping through his notebook. He pulled out a pen and yanked off the top with his teeth.

"You said you saw Dick Richardson recently," he said, the cigar smoke forming a thick haze in the corner of the room.

I nodded my head. "Last week," I said. "He stopped by the plant. We talked for a while."

"What did you talk about?"

"Veal. Do you know how they get it so tender?"

Johnson shook his head no.

"What they do is take the male calves from their mothers immediately after birth. Then they stick 'em in a wooden box, which is designed to prevent any movement. They're fed a diet lacking in any iron, which keeps them anemic and creates the desired pale pink color. Since they crave iron, they usually make do by licking the urine-saturated slats of their stalls. Their muscles slowly begin deteriorating and—"

Johnson interrupted me. "When you spoke. Did things seem normal?"

"Sure," I said. "Normal as hell."

"You got along with him pretty well then?"

"Absolutely. Don't get me wrong. We had our differences like all families, but for the most part we were as close as could be. Richard got me my job over at the rendering plant and later at the slaughterhouse. For that I will be forever grateful."

"And you still work there?"

I shook my head. "It wasn't an easy decision, but I was recently forced to quit. My body was just taking too much abuse. I doubt I'll ever find another job I feel so passionately about. You know what our motto is, don't you? 'Sunshine Foods: Where Quality Means Something.' I believe that Richard, in his genius, conceived that one."

The detective raised one eyebrow and cleared his throat loudly. "He was shot point-blank," he said. "Any enemies you know about?"

I bristled at the suggestion. "There was never a finer man than Richard Richardson, and I'm not saying that just to be talking. It's a fact. To know him was to love and respect him. He was a God-fearing man, a man of principles. Do you know he worked his way up from a lowly meatpacker all the way to Director of Operations? No wait, I'm getting the story mixed up. He took over his old man's job, didn't have to lift a fucking finger. But listen: I'm sure if he hadn't been born into a life of luxury and privilege, he would have worked his rear off to make something of himself. Rest fucking assured."

Johnson pulled the damp cigar from his mouth and crushed it out against the wall. Then he stuck it back into his shirt pocket. His lips tugged upward into a slight grin—or maybe it was just a twitch. "You know a man named Ponso Arguello?"

I shook my head. "Never heard of him. Is he somehow involved?"

Don Johnson coughed into his hand and wiped it clean with his handkerchief. "He and Dick shared a love interest.

Woman named Scarlett Acres. And the body was found in Ponso's SUV. So, yeah, he's a person of great interest."

I rose to my feet, slammed my fist against the chest of drawers with great flare. "Well, Jesus H. Christ. Seems to me that you've got your man."

"Seems that way," he said. "But he's gone missing. Hell of a thing. Might be in Mexico by now."

I shook my head ruefully. "You'll find him," I said. "I'm confident about that."

Johnson asked me some more questions, but I can't remember what they were. Finally, he closed his notebook and nodded his head. "I won't be taking up any more of your time," he said. "Thanks for the lighter. Must have forgotten mine in the car."

"Anytime."

He started toward the door but stopped before opening it. He turned around and frowned. "Tell me again, Frankie. You never heard of Ponso Arguello, huh?"

"No, sir," I said.

He paused for a moment more before nodding his head curtly and leaving. He limped his way through the living room and out the front door, pausing every few steps to cough and wheeze. Looking back now, I should have killed the asthmatic son-of-a-bitch while I still had a chance.

That night, I ordered a meat lover's pizza from Domino's so Ruth wouldn't have to cook. Don't say I'm insensitive. I would have gotten her roses too, but that seemed like a lot of work, going to the flower shop and all. We sat at the dinner table, but it was all doom and gloom. Ruth kept breaking down every few minutes, making it nearly impossible to enjoy my pizza. "He was a good man," she said, her face all red and puffy.

"The finest in the world," I agreed.

"Who would have done something like this? Who?"

"Somebody who was awfully greedy. Or maybe awfully needy."

Seeing as how she wasn't touching her food, I grabbed the last slice of pizza off her plate and stuffed it in my mouth, washing it down with some sewer water they called beer.

"Speaking of money," I said. "You might want to call your father's lawyers. Get the details of his estate hashed out. I assume he had some sort of a will."

Ruth looked up at me disdainfully. "How can you be thinking of money at a time like this?"

I wiped my mouth with a napkin and belched silently. "I'm just trying to be pragmatic," I said. "I've been reading a lot about investing, about how it's important to enter into the marketplace and create a diverse portfolio. Of course, I've always considered myself something of a fiscal conservative, so I want to keep the majority of our upcoming portfolio in safe cash equivalents such as money market funds or CDs. The rest we can invest in a mid-cap fund such as Meridian Growth or Vanguard Selected Value. We should probably stay away from IPOs and high-tech stocks because of their tendency to drop suddenly. And what about investing in gold? I've also considered this option carefully. The gold market is predictably cyclical and is a good indicator on how the rest of the market will react. It also has a better track record than any government's paper currency over the years. And Morningstar's index of gold mining mutual funds is up sixty-six percent after a rise of twenty-one percent the previous year."

Ruth frowned. "I think we should just give the money to the Catholic Church."

I choked on my pizza and had to give myself the Heimlich maneuver to unclog my throat. "What did you say?"

Her green eyes filled with sadness and rage. "Money can't buy happiness," she said.

"It can't buy poverty either."

She bit her lower lip, then started crying again. I just sighed and shook my head.

On the morning of Richard Richardson's funeral, the clouds looked like they were ready to burst, but the rain never came. Instead, there was only thunder, sounding like furniture being dragged across the desert sky. I got dressed in my wedding suit. The sleeves were too short, and the tie was too long, but Ruth still said I looked very handsome.

Maple Hill Funeral Home was located in a town called Pueblo Dinero, which was about forty miles northeast of Huerfano. Pueblo Dinero was a golfer's paradise with dozens of challenging courses scattered across the community. As far as I could tell, only leathery-faced Caucasians were allowed in town, although some Mexicans were granted temporary access to clean their cars, houses, and underwear. I drove through town while Ruth sat in the passenger seat bawling and sniveling. I kept trying to comfort her by saying things like "He's in a better place now" and "He was too good for this world," but that just seemed to make things worse.

The funeral home was a giant contemporary house surrounded by lush grass and a small pond. Water conservation was not an issue in Pueblo Dinero. Rich-looking people were milling outside, shaking hands, conversing, and exchanging business cards. We parked the Chevrolet Beretta in between a Rolls Royce and a Jaguar and started toward the party.

Inside the home it was hot and filled with cautious whispers. The open casket was at the front. I didn't have a burning desire to peek inside. Ruth went by herself, and when she saw his dead face, she burst into tears once more. I stood by the doorway, my suit causing me to sweat. I pulled out a cigarette and lit it. Not two moments later, an old woman in a black sequin dress, who looked like she might be Maple Hill's next paying customer, tapped me on the shoulder and shook her head. "There is no smoking, sir," she said.

"It's not going to do them any harm," I said, and she frowned. Not wanting to make a scene on my father-in-law's big day, I crushed out the cigarette and stuck it in my pocket. I chewed on some tinfoil instead.

The eulogy was given by a priest who resembled God himself: big white beard, booming voice. It was boring as hell, filled with worthless anecdotes and generic proclamations. The only time I woke from my slumber was when he spoke about "the evildoer who committed the heinous acts that ended Richard's life." He promised that God's judgment would be swift and harsh, and that the murderer would end up burning among the fiery brimstones of hell. I only hoped they would have the courtesy to leave me freshly laundered towels on my bed of coal.

After the service, I helped carry Dick's coffin from the funeral home to the hearse. People bowed their heads in respect as we walked past, and I grinned cheerfully. "A lot of dead weight," I commented to a toupee-wearing old man. Ruth and I got to ride in one of the hearses. Outside, townspeople stopped at street corners and watched the procession move slowly through town. I felt like a celebrity.

At the cemetery, the wind started blowing pretty hard, kicking up dust, and when the priest spoke, his words were muffled and hard to hear. He asked everybody to bow their heads and say a prayer for Dick. I bowed my head, but I didn't know what to say. Eventually, the priest nodded solemnly at Ruth and handed her a shovel. She dug some dirt from the ground and tossed it into the hole. The moment the soil scattered across the coffin, she released an anguished cry, covering her mouth with her hand. People were born and people died.

As we were leaving, I noticed a young man standing at the edge of the graveyard grounds, partially obscured by a tree. I walked toward him and we made eye contact. His face was badly deformed. He had a cleft palate, two misshaped eyes, and a head shaped like a peanut. But it wasn't his appearance that caused my body to stiffen. Beneath all the malformation was a palpable meanness, a rage. Fear rose up inside of me. My mouth opened and three strange words escaped: "I know you," I said. The freak nodded his head, then turned around and limped away on clubbed feet, disappearing into the windswept dust.

CHAPTER 16

The next couple of days passed like nameless corpses. I slept. I ate. I watched bad television. I talked with condescending lawyers who thought I couldn't tell my dick from a garden hose. Depression was gnawing at my brain. Finally, on Tuesday morning, I decided that Phase Two of Operation What's Owed to Me needed to commence.

Outside, hell's diamond was shining in the sapphire sky. I crawled into my Beretta, hit the engine, and drove. The streets were deserted. It was as if the world had ended, but they'd forgotten to tell me.

Marteau had suggested I pay a Dr. Burroughs a visit. He worked out of his house, a small lime-green stucco-ranch surrounded by a collapsing metal fence. A poodle with a lampshade around its neck was yapping at a three-legged cat stuck in a tree. On the front porch stood a fully ornamented Christmas tree, and hanging from the roof were icicle lights. The lawn was filled with life-sized plywood cutouts of Santa Claus, elves, toy soldiers, Jesus Christ, and Frosty the Snowman. Hanging from the side of the house was an oversized banner that read "Have Yourself a Merry Little Christmas." It wasn't August yet.

I walked unsteadily toward the house. I stood on the front porch. The door opened before I had a chance to knock. A dwarf of a man stood in the doorway wearing a white doctor's jacket and holding a thick book called *The Primate's Brain*. He had gray hair and a round jolly face. "You must be Frankie," he said. "Jack told me you might be coming."

Inside the house, a ceiling fan was wheezing and groaning. Several aquariums filled with snakes and spiders and newts were lined on the mantel. There was no furniture but plenty of strange objects: an old typewriter, a human skeleton, a sewing machine, a ventriloquist doll, a brass teakettle. There was a built-in bookshelf filled with DVDs. I glanced at some of the titles: *Forrest Hump*, *Sperms of Endearment*, *Sex-Starved Fuck Sluts #24*, *Sushi Girls* and *Stir-Fry Snatch*, just to name a few.

Dr. Burroughs offered me a chair—actually an empty whiskey carton—while he lit up a joint. Then he paced back and forth across the room, while I sat there feeling more than a little uncomfortable.

"I don't know why I'm here," I said.

He laughed, but the laughter was too brief to show any humor. "You've got a problem," he said, "You need my help."

"What problem?" I said.

"You need your wife dead, no?"

I didn't say anything, although I might have nodded.

"You've shown yourself very capable in the act of murder. But in this case, a violent death would spark suspicions about your involvement. Might even force the detectives to refocus the Richard Richardson case. Might allow them to discover the truth about Ponso Arguello and José Gutierrez."

"Yes," I said.

"And that's why you're here."

"Yes," I said. "That's why I'm here."

Burroughs placed his joint in an ashtray. Then he reached into one of the aquariums and pulled out a newt. He placed it on his wrist and watched in apparent fascination as the little creature crawled up his skin. He looked at me, his eyes magnified behind his thick spectacles. "Would you care to see my credentials?" he said.

I shook my head. "Nah. That's okay."

"I'm not a quack, if that's what you were thinking. I was educated at Johns Hopkins."

I shifted uneasily in my seat. "So what are we gonna do?"

A thin grin spread across Burroughs's face. He placed the newt back in the aquarium and tossed in a couple of food pellets. "They're very good nowadays," he said, "at determining cause of death. Making a homicide appear to be a suicide is tricky business, Frankie, very tricky business indeed."

"Can you help me or not?"

He took a step forward and licked his lips. "I don't know you, Frankie, don't know you at all. You seem to be a rather distasteful young man if you don't mind my saying. But Jack Marteau is a dear friend of mine. And when a dear friend asks for a favor..."

Dr. Burroughs disappeared into the back of his house. When he returned, he was holding a leather tote bag in one hand and a doctor's needle in the other. He squeezed out some liquid and grinned. "This lovely concoction is a creation of Sam Burroughs M.D. I'm quite proud of it. It's a simple cocktail of legal prescription drugs. Methadone, Lexapro, Zoloft, choral hydrate. I have found it to be very effective in situations like yours. The key is finding a good vein. You might wait until she's asleep. It won't take long. The death will be painless, quite pleasant actually. The drugs will be found in her system. The same drugs I prescribed for her depression. It will be ruled an accident-tal overdose. No problem."

"Sounds simple enough…"

He opened the leather bag. It was filled with several written prescriptions and empty vials of medication. "Scatter the prescriptions and vials throughout the bedroom," he said. "The authorities will question me. You need not worry. I will convince them. I'm very forceful when I have to be. It will be an open-and-shut case. You will win in the end, Frankie."

That night I held Ruth tight and felt every breath she took. Off in the distance, a police siren wailed. It was the most lonesome sound I'd ever heard.

I couldn't sleep. And I couldn't bring myself to do it while she was sleeping. It was strange. I went into the kitchen and made myself a snack. Toast with mustard. Beer with gin. I ate quickly and vomited in the sink. I dropped a new package of Marlboros on the kitchen table. I pulled one out and stuck it in my mouth. I couldn't find my lighter. I got out of my chair and used the gas stove to light it. I nearly singed my eyebrows. For the next hour or so I sat at the kitchen table smoking cigarettes and reading the funny pages. Dagwood was up to his usual crazy antics, running late for work and knocking over the mailman, while poor Charlie Brown was getting fooled again by that bitch Lucy. When would he ever learn? Never trust a woman.

I returned to the bedroom and sat down on a chair. The sun was rising. I watched Ruth sleep. Eventually she started stirring. She stretched her obese body, and her eyes fluttered open. When she saw me sitting there, she smiled. "You're up early," she said in a drowsy voice. "You couldn't sleep?"

I shook my head. "I've got a lot on my mind."

I got to my feet and walked over to the bed. I hovered over Ruth. Light was filtering in through the curtains, and there were strange shadows on the wall. Ruth sat up in bed and wiped the mess of hair from her face. "Is something wrong, Frankie?" she said. "You seem a little off."

I shook my head. "We don't have a choice, do we?"

"Choice about what? What are you talking about?"

"We do all sorts of strange things, and we never know why, not for sure. Stealing. Raping. Killing. Where'd we learn this wickedness? From our parents, right? Look at the way they treated us, for Christ's sake! Dad beating us with a belt for wetting our beds. Mom chaining us to a fence post, making us drink and eat out of dog bowls. And Uncle Sal, good ol' Uncle Sal, burning us with cigarettes when we stutter, trying to break us of the habit. Blame our parents. Our teachers. Our priests. That's why we're so fucked up. And don't think I haven't tried. But it doesn't work, Ruthie, it doesn't work. We just end up with more questions. Like why did they do those cruel things? Because of their parents? Or their parents' parents? You keep going from generation to generation, but it just doesn't work. Nasty cycle, you see. So what are we left with? Who made us evil? Who's been injecting this malevolence into our skulls while we're sleeping? Isn't the answer clear? Hallelujah, praise God! For he made us in his own image, hideous image that it is."

"Frankie," Ruth said, her lower lip trembling. "You're scaring me. You're not making any sense."

I sat down on the corner of the bed and shook my head, holding back the tears welling up deep within my soul. "Why'd you have to do it?" I asked, my voice filling with some long-lost emotion.

Ruth furrowed her brow and squinted her eyes. "Why did I have to do what?" she said.

"Why'd you have to go and kill yourself?"

She shook her head. She still didn't get it. "Kill myself?"

"You had so much going for you," I said. "Couldn't you have held on just a little bit longer?"

Ruth laughed apprehensively. I grabbed a hold of her hand and squeezed until she grimaced in pain. "I was looking forward to our new life together. I was ready to move to the suburbs, ready to live the American dream. Three-thousand-square-foot house, three-car garage, self-cleaning oven. The whole bit. But then I came home and found you lying on the bed staring at the ceiling with those empty pill bottles scattered at your feet. Look at what you left behind. All the laughter and tears and kisses and hope and heartache..."

An expression of uneasiness spread across Ruth's face. She rose from the bed and tried to get to her feet, but I wouldn't let her. I shoved her back down and shrieked. "Frankie, please," she said. "Don't do this. Don't hurt me."

"Why not?" I said. "Why the fuck not?"

"Because...because you love me."

The comment was so humorous I almost wet myself.

"Love you?" I said. "Well, I'll say this much. If I loved good-for-nothing whores, I'd hug you so hard you'd need to buy a new spine at the five-and-dime store."

Ruth couldn't respond. She could only babble. "Frankie...no...I...you." The madmen orchestra started playing in my head. Brass and strings and percussion. The time was now. I sprung on top of her and pinned her down. I cocked my arm back and slammed my fist into her stomach. It was like punching a ton of fresh dough. She gasped. I continued pounding on her, pounding on her, until my arm was tired and my fingers were sore. Ruth was sobbing, but I couldn't stop laughing. It was terrible. This was no time for pleasure.

You never think they're gonna fight back, but sometimes they do. Ruth kneed me in the groin. It didn't bother me. I slapped her across the face. I had to be careful. I didn't want to leave any marks. But when she bit my hand, causing me to bleed, I became entrapped by a lethal mix of anxiety and rage. I grabbed her by the throat and squeezed. Her eyes bulged as she tried futilely to pry my fingers away. Aside from my own grunts, everything was silent. Ruth's eyes remained open as her face turned red and then purple. She continued struggling, her legs kicking and her fingers scratching weakly at my forearms. As her resistance slowed, I released my grip and she collapsed spread-eagle on the mattress, gasping for breath.

The rope I'd purchased was under the bed. I cut off a section and proceeded to bind the fat lady's feet together. I'd learned two things in Boy Scouts, and tying ropes was one of them. I don't remember what the other thing was.

The oxygen was returning to Ruth's brain, and she was

beginning to blink. She didn't know where she was or what the fuck was going on. I tied her hands. She was immobilized. And then I pulled out the needle. Ruth seemed to regain her senses. Her eyes opened wide and she started flopping around like a fish on a rowboat. I told her to calm down, to just calm down, that it would make things easier, but they never listen to reason now, do they?

As I pressed the needle against her skin, Ruth started begging and cursing and screaming and crying. I didn't look at her face. I would have lost the nerve. I'm only human. I jammed the needle into her neck and squeezed out the medicine.

When the operation was complete, I walked across the room and sat on the chair. I closed my eyes, and listened to the screams—horrible screams—echoing throughout the room. Eventually the screams became softer and more muffled. Then they stopped altogether.

CHAPTER 17

I went to the living room and lay on the couch. I fell asleep right away. I had strange dreams that made no sense, random firing of synapses. When I woke up, I was confused. I wasn't sure if I'd really done what I'd done. I returned to the bedroom. Ruth was dead. I cursed and shook my head. It was a fucking shame life had to be this nasty. I stood there for quite a while, my hands trembling badly. Then I untied her hands and feet.

The phone rang. I picked up the receiver and grunted.

"Frankie. It's Jack Marteau. Is the job done?"

"Yeah," I said. "It's done."

"You need somebody to talk to. It's not wise to keep your emotions bottled up inside."

"Says you."

"Tell me. Do you know where the Most Precious Blood Church is?"

"I haven't been to church since I was baptized against my will."

"It's at the north end of Main, right past the railroad tracks. Meet me there in an hour."

"You sure a church is going to be open at this hour?"

He chuckled. "I know some people there. I'll have them leave the door open for us."

* * *

Outside, the moon was drowning in a sea of tar. A day-old newspaper tiptoed through the gutter, and I kicked it along its way. I stuck my hands in my pocket and trudged toward my car. I got inside and hit the engine. I turned on the radio. Tanya Tucker was singing. I hated Tanya Tucker.

I drove through the streets of Huerfano. Everybody in town was dead. A corpse in a gray wig stood on the porch in her white nightgown, beating a rug against the cement. A skeleton wearing an A-frame undershirt sat at his kitchen table, his head bowed, while in the living room his murdered wife lay on a couch and watched television, the laugh track echoing through the morgue-house. An aborted child flew through the air on a swing in a grave-yard of a playground. A deceased woman kneeled in front of St. Peter's Church, fondling a rosary and mumbling a thousand unanswered prayers. Our stars and our moon and our God. All dead. And me. Just another hell-bound soul waiting for deliverance.

I stopped into a joint on North Main called Eddie's Tavern for a quick drink. I hadn't been there in years. The neon sign was flickering, like some grade-B noir movie. A couple of pickups were parked outside the front of the bar. One of them had a flat tire. I entered the bar. My boots echoed on the wooden floor. Above the pyramid of liquor bottles, a television was turned on, but there was no sound. Aside from the bartender, there was only one other person in the place: an old woman with blue hair and orange skin. She was talking to herself, obviously quite soused. The bartender was a middle-aged Indian with a puffy red nose and a despondent expression. "Two Budweisers and two shots of vodka," I said, reaching for my wallet.

"You 'specting someone?"

"Now why would you say that?"

He shook his head slowly and fetched me my drinks. Meanwhile, the old lady continued to jabber away, a bucket of saliva dribbling down her chin. "You can't go into them outhouses no more," she said. "They's got cameras down there. They's watchin' you all the time."

I smiled at the crazy bitch and downed my first beer. Then I chased it down with my first shot of vodka. I nodded at the sad Indian. "Does Doug still own this place?"

"No, Doug is dead."

"How'd he die?" I asked.

"I don't know, he just died. I guess it was two years ago. Just died."

As if on cue, the jukebox started up, playing "Graveyard Waltz" by the Hooters. I rested my head against my hand. I was tired. Goddamn tired. As tired as an anemic anaconda after eating an oversized antelope. I closed my eyes for a moment. When I opened them, the crazy old lady was sitting right next to me. She smelled like gin-drenched mothballs. "Have you ever been inside somebody's head?" she whispered into my ear. "It's a goddamn house of mirrors." Her hideous laughter trailed me out the door.

The Most Precious Blood Church of Christ was a small square brick building with a steel door and a red awning.

I did the sign of the cross and entered.

Inside it was dark except for a few large candles flickering. At the front of the church was an extraordinarily bloody crucifix. The ground beneath my feet was cement, as were the "pews." A scorpion scurried across the floor and disappeared into a crack.

Marteau was sitting in the front row, his hat on his lap, his briefcase at his feet. His eyes were closed, and for a moment I thought he might be praying. But then he turned his head quickly and rose to his feet. "Frankie," he said. "So good to see you."

I sat down next to him and stared at the torn body of Christ. The salesman placed his icy hand on my shoulder. An uneasy feeling spread through my body, zigzagging around my joints and ligaments and cartilage. Marteau moved even closer so that I could feel his breath on my neck.

"Tell me about it," he said. "Tell me all about it."

"Not much to tell," I said. "The corpses are piling up."

"Are you having second thoughts?"

"I feel like I'm disappearing," I said. "Like my soul is collapsing on itself."

He laughed vindictively and squeezed my arm. "Listen to me, Frankie. Listen closely. You're changing, changing for the better. As a boy you always played the passive victim, didn't you? Oh perhaps there were a few occasions where you lashed out with your fists trying to make them recognize you, but that rage was always directed generally, abstractly, not the necessary focused resistance. But now things are different. You've become a man. You've become a force to be reckoned with. Your soul's not disappearing. It's becoming more powerful. I did my research, Frankie. You think I picked you by accident?"

"Picked me? What the hell are you talking about?"

"Killing comes easy, doesn't it? This is what you were born to do."

"You're the one," I shouted, the volume of my voice surprising me. "You're the one who told me to do it. You told me to kill Richard Richardson. You told me to kill Ruth."

"I did nothing of the kind. And what about Ponso Arguello? Or José Gutierrez? Are you going to blame those killings on me as well? Well, are you? But why are we arguing? What is done is done. Now we must look toward the future."

"No," I heard myself say. "I don't want any more of your help. I'm in too deep. Maybe I should confess, confess to all of it. Maybe I can still be saved…"

"And go back to prison? You can't do it, Frankie. We both know it. Let me help you."

"To hell with you," I said, but my voice was faltering.

The salesman's lips slithered into a terrible grin. He squeezed my arm tighter. His grip was like a vise. "You know who I am, don't you, Frankie? You've always known."

"No," I said. "Leave me alone."

His eyes narrowed into slits. "I'm the sound of a midnight train. I'm the chill that runs up your spine. I'm the quickening of your heartbeat. I'm the shiver on a winter's night. I've been around, Frankie. I've been around longer than you know."

"I'm getting out of here," I said and began to rise, but Marteau didn't let go of my wrist, and with surprising strength, pulled me back down.

"I met your Scarlett Acres," he said. "The resemblance is uncanny. She looks exactly like your mother."

"Fuck you."

"And just imagine, Frankie. Once you get Richard Richardson's money, once you get all of Richard Richardson's money, Mommy will be all yours. You'll be able to fuck her up the ass all day long. Just fuck her and fuck her and listen to her squeal like the little swine she is."

I lost control. I grabbed Marteau by the throat and punched him several times in the kidneys. But instead of doubling over in pain, he only laughed, an evil chortle, and that made me even madder. I dragged him from the pew and threw him onto the cement floor. He placed his hands into the air, asked me to stop, please, please stop, all the while giggling like a Saigon whore. But I didn't stop. I pounded his head against the ground and heard his skull crack open. Blood drained from his ears, but his eyes remained lively and alert. "Very much like a cockroach," he said. "Amazing. Truly amazing."

It didn't matter what I did to him. I hit him. I kicked him. I stomped on him. I bit him. He just continued to laugh and call me names (although every once in a while the laughter changed to tears as he sang Irish drinking songs.)

After ten or so minutes, the anger had finally drained out of my veins. I pushed his bloodied body away from me and sat down on the ground, pulling my legs toward my chest.

"Why are you doing this?" I cried. "What do you want from me?"

Marteau pulled himself to his feet and wiped the dirt and blood off his arms. "We can discuss payment at another time. What's important is that you don't give up on yourself. Not now. Follow that dream, young man. Follow that dream." He stuck out his hand and helped me to my feet. I felt another burst of rage. Without a second thought, I cocked my arm back and swung wildly, smashing my fist against his gaunt face. He crumpled to the ground.

"You are incorrigible, young Frankie, absolutely incorrigible."

I stumbled out of the church, the steel door slamming shut behind me.

CHAPTER 18

The coroner ruled it an overdose, just like Dr. Burroughs had promised. But Detective Johnson was skeptical. Less than a week after her death, he showed up at my front porch wearing a white short-sleeved dress shirt soaked through with perspiration. He was patting his forehead down with a handkerchief. Dried saliva was caked onto the corners of his mouth. A badly wounded cigar protruded from his shirt pocket.

"I need to talk to you," Johnson rasped.

"I'm in the middle of something. I could come by the station—"

"I need to talk to you."

I didn't argue further. He followed me inside. I could hear him wheezing. I sat down on the couch, crossed my legs, and folded my hands behind my head. Like I was the most relaxed son-of-a-bitch west of the Pacific Ocean. Johnson pulled out his cigar and put a match to it. He puffed for thirty seconds or more before the thing lit. Then he sat down on a folding metal chair and glared at me. "Shame about your wife," he said.

"Yeah, thanks," I said. "Sometimes I don't know how I'm going to go on. Guess I just have to take it day by day, you know?"

He hacked a few times, covering his mouth with his

filthy handkerchief. "It's the only way," he finally said.

I straightened up on the couch and squinted. "So what do you need to talk to me about, Detective?"

Johnson bit down on his cigar, baring a set of tobacco-stained teeth. He cleared his throat. "Your wife. Her death."

"Not much to tell," I said. "Worst thing I ever saw. Doubt I'll ever be able to get the image out of my head."

"Must be plenty tough."

"The loss is unfathomable. I can't help but blame myself. If I had paid closer attention to her suffering, to her torment, maybe I could have done…something."

Johnson half grinned; I guess you could call it a smirk. "Don't beat yourself up, Frank. You've suffered plenty."

"I suppose you're right—"

"But at least you've got some spending money now. That inheritance should help ease some of the pain, don't you think?"

"I'll be able to pay the rent, if that's what you're asking."

Johnson's dark beady eyes narrowed into slits, and sweat glistened on the top of his bald head. "You think I'm an idiot?"

"I don't know you well enough to answer confidently."

"Here's the thing. Your wife didn't commit suicide."

"That's a lie," I said. "She was depressed. After her old man died, she became ensnared in a vacuum of melancholy. She didn't see a way out. She'd been seeing a psychiatrist. Dr. Burroughs is his name. He gave her a few prescriptions. She swallowed as many as she could. Died in her sleep. Painless."

Johnson shook his head. "Not so painless," he said.

"There were bruises on her face and on her neck. She didn't do that to herself, Frankie."

The color drained from my face, but I kept it together. Johnson was bluffing, trying to get me to bite. If he'd had anything on me, he'd have already slapped the cuffs across my wrists. "But the coroner said—"

"Fuck the coroner."

"I will if she's attractive."

He laughed hoarsely and dropped his cigar on the floor. He crushed it out with a frayed dress shoe. "Didn't you know that you'd be the first person we'd investigate? Didn't you know that you'd be suspect number one?"

"I didn't kill anybody, if that's what you're suggesting," I said forcefully.

"You quit your job," he said.

"That's not a crime."

"You were tired of waiting. You saw the opportunity."

"You're wrong," I said. "I wouldn't ever hurt anybody, especially my wife."

Johnson placed both of his beefy hands on his knees and leaned forward like a wild animal ready to pounce. "I've seen your record," he growled. "And I've seen the pictures of what you did to that fellow down in Tucson. They should have put you away for longer."

"They got the wrong guy," I said. "The judge had it out for me."

"A victim, huh?"

"I've never felt sorry for myself, not for a single second."

"Sure, Frankie, sure." He rose to his feet, coughed a few times, and glared brutally at poor old me. "One other thing. Last time we talked. You said you'd never met Ponso Arguello."

"That's right."

"I've got about a half dozen witnesses that say otherwise."

"But none of them are as trustworthy as me, I bet."

"They say you were making a play for his girlfriend. This Scarlett Acres. They say he gave you a couple of beat-downs."

"They must have me confused with somebody else. Like I said, I don't know anybody named Ponso. And I don't know anybody named Scarlett either."

Johnson hacked some more and soothed himself with his inhaler. "Do me a favor," he said. "Don't leave Huerfano. It's only a matter of time now."

"I'm not going anywhere," I said. "I'm chained to this goddamn town by the shoulder blades."

Beluga caviar, wild boar pâté, and winter black truffles.

But the money didn't come.

Brioni suits, black ostrich shoes, and dazzling porcelain veneers.

But the money didn't come.

Quail hunting, recreational drug use, and zero to sixty in four-point-nine seconds.

But the money didn't come. The fucking money didn't come.

Scarlett invited me to her house. She was lonely with Ponso gone. When I arrived, she was sitting on the front porch twirling her hair and sucking on a lollipop. I liked that. She was wearing a pink jogging suit, the top unzipped just far enough to make me excited. When she saw me, she smiled or sneered, it was always hard to tell with her.

"Frankie, Frankie, you look so frazzled. Not sleeping well?"

"I'm sleeping just fine."

"So? Are you gonna take me away? Are we going to live happily ever after? The stripper and the meatpacker?"

I spat on the ground and wiped the perspiration from my forehead. "These things take time. In the interim, we should be careful. Not be seen together. Not look too happy. Those types of things."

She stuck her lollipop back in her mouth and crunched it with her teeth. "I'm getting a bad vibe from you, Frankie. I keep thinking you're gonna take the money and run, leave me all alone."

I pulled out a cigarette and bit off the filter. "Now that's crazy talk," I said. "Money in and of itself is worthless. It's what you can buy with the money that means something. And you're what I can buy with the money."

"Is that supposed to be sweet?"

"It's supposed to be the truth."

Scarlett's chin slumped forward, her badly dyed hair falling over her eyes. "How much longer, Frankie? Tell me the truth."

"Won't be long now. We've just got to be a little patient. There's just a lot of red tape. I haven't even gotten my wife in the ground yet."

"The one you killed?"

"Jesus, Scarlett. Don't say that. It was suicide. She was devastated."

"Suicide. Beautiful. And her father was killed by a jealous boyfriend."

"Yeah. As far as they know. But what are you getting so angry for?"

"I'm not angry," she said, her voice suddenly tender. Or as tender as a whore could get. "I'm afraid."

"Afraid of what?"

"Lots of things. Being alone. Dying poor. And you. I'm afraid of you."

"Oh come on. I'm a pussycat. I only did what I did to make a better life for you and me. Besides. The world is a better place without them. All of them."

"Maybe…"

I pulled her close, kissed her on the forehead. "Stop worrying," I said. "Everything's gonna be all right." And for a moment I might have even believed it.

The weeks passed and nothing much happened. Ruth was given a proper funeral and buried in a plot next to her father. The search for Ponso Arguello lost momentum. The tragic newspaper stories about Richard Richardson and his daughter ceased, replaced by happier stories about county fairs and gang rapes. Don Johnson left me alone, although I know for a fact he was keeping tabs on me.

Nights were hard. I couldn't sleep. This one particular night I was sitting in the living room watching television, feeling good and depressed. I tried for nostalgia. Carving pumpkins with my mother at the kitchen table while the autumn leaves fall lazily to the ground. Sledding down a steep hill, the snowflakes landing on my tongue. Tossing a baseball with my father, knowing smiles on our faces as the ball smacks against the leather. Sitting by the lake on a lazy summer afternoon, watching the tadpoles dart through the water. I sucked down some smoke and closed my eyes. Times that had never happened. The truth was, I didn't have a single happy memory I could extract from my brain. I grinned bitterly.

The show I wasn't watching ended. I turned off the television. I sat there, staring straight ahead. Then I heard footsteps just outside the front door. I stiffened. There was some rattling. Then I saw something appear beneath the door. A manila envelope. I heard the footsteps again. This time moving quickly. A few moments passed. A car door slammed. Then the car screeched away.

Twenty minutes passed, maybe more. I didn't move. I stared at the envelope. Off in the distance the lonely cry of a train warned people to get the hell out of its way. I rose to my feet. I felt light-headed. I needed a drink. It took me a month to walk across the living room. My feet kept getting stuck to the floor. I squatted on my knees and picked up the envelope. My name was written on the front. My hands were trembling. I begged them to stop. They didn't. I tore a corner off the envelope. Then I used my index finger to pull it completely open. There was a single paper inside. I pulled it out. It was written in red calligraphy. I read it a few times, my mind taking a moment to comprehend. *"You've done some naughty things and the dead are ready to speak. I need ten thousand to keep my mouth shut. I'll contact you on Wednesday at midnight and tell you where to drop the money. You naughty, naughty boy."*

The paper fell out of my hand and floated to the floor. The room started spinning. I tried grabbing hold of the wall, but it was no use. I collapsed to the floor, gritting my teeth so hard that they crumbled in my mouth.

CHAPTER 19

Don't think I didn't suspect her. She was the first person who crossed my deteriorating mind. And if it were true, if my love reincarnate were betraying me, all hell was bound to break loose...

I tried rationalizing her innocence. After all, I'd told her time and time again that I didn't have the money. She could see with her own green eyes that I didn't have the money. I was driving a Beretta, not a Ferrari. I was paying with loose change, not hundred-dollar bills. And even if she suspected that I was somehow hoarding the inheritance, she wouldn't go so far as to blackmail me. Would she?

Of course, Scarlett wasn't the only possibility. There was Marilyn Cook. Or Simon Harris. Or Jack Marteau. They all knew some dark secrets. And they were all capable and willing to make me pay.

My options were limited. I could ignore the demand, assume my tormenter was bluffing. After all, what possible evidence could she have? Photographs? Taped conversations? A witness? Doubtful all. But what if she did have something on me? What if she gave Detective Johnson the break he needed? I couldn't take that chance. Not after all I'd been through. I needed to get the money. Ten thousand dollars. I'd pay her. And then I'd find out who she was. That's the thing about me. I don't forget or forgive those people who have hurt me. I give 'em what they deserve. An eye for an eye and then some.

The next morning I went to visit Daniel Savoy. He was one of the lawyers assigned to Dick's estate. His office was in Johnstown, smack middle in a strip mall. His secretary was a fifty-something former prom queen with a page-boy hairdo. "Can I help you?" she said in a voice full of heartache.

"I need to speak with Daniel Savoy."

"Do you have an appointment?"

"No. But it won't take but a minute. I'm Frankie Avicious and I've got some money coming my way. Big money."

"I'll see if he's busy," she said. "Have a seat."

I sat down in the waiting room, picked up a copy of the *Sports Illustrated* swimsuit issue. Read the articles. After a few minutes, the secretary said, "Mr. Savoy will see you now."

Daniel Savoy was tall and skinny and had bushy black hair. He wore a shiny gray suit and a too-short tie. His blue eyes were unaffected, and he had a strange habit of licking his lower lip each time he spoke. We shook hands and he patted me on the shoulder with his free hand, said, "I know it's a terrible time for you."

"You have no idea," I said.

He sat down at the edge of the desk, gestured me to sit on the chair. "What can I help you with, Mr. Avicious?"

"It's about the money," I said. "The inheritance money."

"Yes?"

"I just wanted to clarify. That money is rightfully mine, isn't it?"

Savoy nodded stiffly. "It certainly appears that way. As you know, Dick Richardson had left the majority of his estate to his daughter. While the transference had not yet taken place, the estate was lawfully under her ownership. Of course, her passing complicated things. As far as we know, Ruth had not drawn up a will. If a will is not discovered, then Arizona law stipulates that the spouse takes full ownership."

"Yeah, right. Well, I need that money pronto."

Savoy rose from his desk and walked across the room. He straightened out a painting on the wall, then turned and faced me. "You do understand that these circumstances are somewhat unique, don't you, Mr. Avicious?"

"What circumstances are you referring to?"

"Your father-in-law was murdered. And before your wife ever saw a dime of the inheritance, she died herself, rather mysteriously."

"What are you implying, sir?"

He grinned, but his eyes remained cold. "I'm not implying a thing. I only hope you understand this situation will take quite some time to get resolved."

I clenched my fists. I was getting agitated. "How long are we talking?"

"Months," he said. "Maybe even years."

"Years? You're shitting me."

"As I said, the circumstances are quite unique. And it's a lot of money..."

"Well, here's the thing," I said, flashing a good-natured grin of my own. "I don't need all the money. Not now anyway. I just need a portion, say ten thousand dollars. See, I owe somebody some money and—"

"I'm sorry, Mr. Avicious. There's nothing I can do. If you're interested in applying for an inheritance loan, I can help you fill out the paperwork. Other than that…"

I rose to my feet and shoved the chair to the ground. "Fuck a loan," I said. "That money belongs to me. Who the fuck do you think you are, hoarding my money?"

"I'm going to have to ask you to leave, Mr. Avicious."

"I'm leaving," I said, knocking some papers off the bloodsucker's desk. "But I'll be back soon, and I'm getting my goddamn money. I've worked too fucking hard, come too fucking far."

I stormed out of his office, kicking the floor and punching the walls. The secretary smiled at me. "Have a happy day," she said.

The next couple of days were a toilet bowl full of diarrhea. I withdrew all remaining funds from my bank account. Twelve hundred dollars and change. I hawked my wedding band and my baseball cards. I sold my furniture and bed and television. I slept on the floor and watched the shadows on the walls.

I called up old friends. I didn't have many. I told them I needed money for a surgery. Frontal lobotomy. They all hung up on me. Except for an old pal named Chester. He took pity on me. He gave me a hundred fifty bucks and a gift certificate to The Three Little Piggies Restaurant. That's where he worked. It was the best he could do.

So what next? I wandered the streets, begging for loose change or diamonds. I checked the change slot in pay phones and vending machines. I sold plasma at the blood bank.

When all was said and done, I had a little more than five thousand dollars. Not bad for two days' work, but far short of the necessary funds. There was nothing else to do. I wasn't about to rob a bank. I was an honest man.

I met with Scarlett at the No-Tel Motel. I wanted to feel her out on this whole blackmailing thing. At first I made a halfhearted attempt at romance, but she wasn't in the mood. Said she wasn't feeling well. Couldn't stop throwing up. I offered her a bottle of tequila. Sometimes that works for me. She declined.

So I got to the subject at hand. "How you doing for money these days?" I asked. "Getting enough to eat?"

"Sure."

"That's good. Me, I'm in a little bind. Seems that somebody's blackmailing me. Putting a real crimp in my mourning process."

Scarlett looked genuinely surprised. Her jaw actually dropped. But she was a stripper. Pretending came easy. "Blackmailing you? What are you talking about?"

"Someone slipped a note under my door. He's threatening to blow things up. Unless I hand over a large sum of money."

"No shit, Frankie?"

"No shit. Now if I had the money, I wouldn't be so goddamn stressed. I'd consider it a luxury tax. But I haven't gotten a dime yet. Bureaucracy and such. Do you believe me, Scarlett? I haven't gotten a dime."

"Of course I believe you," she said. "But can't you... can't you get some of the money? I mean it's yours, isn't it?"

"That's what I thought. But the lawyers are like cockroaches. You can cut off their heads, and they keep marching."

Scarlett rubbed the side of her face. "So what are you gonna do, Frankie?"

"I haven't decided."

"Can you ask your little blackmailer for an extension?"

"Like at tax time? I don't think that's how it works. Besides, the lawyer made it sound as if it might take a while. Years even."

Panic. But she managed to stay cool. "That's bad, Frankie. That's real bad."

"Yeah," I said. "It's a good thing you're marrying me for love and not for the money. Otherwise we'd have a situation, you know?"

I was feeling Scarlett out, and she was feeling me out. Two light heavyweights, early rounds. "What about the blackmailer?" she said. "Do you think he'll follow through? Do you think he's got any real evidence?"

"I think he might."

"Shit, Frankie."

I pulled out a cigarette and lit it. In the room next to ours a couple was fucking or fighting, I couldn't tell which. I waited until the screaming died down. "You know something else I've been thinking?"

"What?"

"I've been thinking that maybe my blackmailer isn't a he."

"A woman?"

"Yeah. In fact, I've even been thinking that maybe my blackmailer is a you."

"What?"

"You just strike me as something of an opportunist, that's all. Fucking your way to the bottom."

Scarlett slapped me across the face. It felt good. I didn't want her to miss out, so I slapped her back. The vein in her forehead bulged and her left eye twitched. "You disgust me. You're a misogynist."

"What'd you call me?"

"A misogynist. A hater of women."

"No, Scarlett, you've got me figured all wrong. I don't hate women. I love 'em. You know what you tell a woman with two black eyes?"

"What?"

"Nothing, you've already tried telling her twice."

It was a good joke, but Scarlett didn't think so. She pulled back her hair, vomited on my lap, and stormed out the door. Me, I lay back in bed and dreamed about hell.

CHAPTER 20

I've always been a sentimental guy. I like long walks along the beach, especially at sunrise, Puccini operas, and Barbra Streisand movies. Okay, I'm lying to you. I like eating and boozing and whoring and killing. What's it to you? But whatever my nature, don't you think I should have been given the opportunity to mourn in the proper way for my deceased wife? I should have been able to stare at our wedding photo for hours at a time forcing tears and feigning misery. I should have been able to sit in a Best Western motel room and count my thousand-dollar bills in peace and quiet without having to deal with conniving lawyers and suspicious detectives and blackmailing mistresses. But that's what I was faced with. With all that external pressure, you might think I would have gotten all rattled and bent out of shape, but I stayed just as cool as could be. A lower power was guiding my every move, my every word. Sometimes you just have to close your eyes and submit to the will of He Who Guides Us.

Time limped along with a tourniquet wrapped around its leg. Then it was Wednesday night. Midnight, I'd be getting another letter. I needed to have ten thousand dollars. I was forty-eight hundred dollars short. These problems arise. I tried calling Marteau. Figured he might have some guidance. I couldn't reach him. His number had been disconnected.

I sat on the couch in blue jeans and an A-frame undershirt soaked through with sweat. I stared at the clock. The seconds ticked away like Chinese water torture. The lights were off and the moonlight filtered through the curtains. My mind was a highway radio station, all full of faraway voices and static.

Midnight. No letter. Twelve-oh-five. No letter. Maybe she'd had second thoughts. Twelve-ten. Nothing. Twelve-fifteen. I rose to my feet. And that's when I heard three loud knocks on the door. They were the only sounds in the world. I raced to the door and kicked it open. I looked around, but she'd vanished into the night. Parked out front was a purple El Camino, the engine running. On the ground was an envelope smeared with lipstick or blood. Hands trembling, I tore open the envelope. The note was written in the same classic calligraphy. It read, *"Stick the money under the passenger seat. Drive to the Huerfano Landfill dumping point. Honk three times. Then walk home. Life keeps getting better."*

Cursing, I stuffed the letter into my jeans pocket. I went into the bedroom and gathered up the money, which was packed in a beer box. I pulled on a flannel shirt, torn at the shoulder, and made my way outside.

The moon looked like a clown smile. Everything was dark. I walked slowly toward the El Camino. I pulled open the driver's-side door and stepped inside. I took a deep breath. Then I jammed the car into gear and pressed slowly on the accelerator.

I drove down County Line Road 5. Everything was so uniformly dark that sometimes I began doubting I was still on the road. Only when it curved and the towering saguaros shimmered in the glow of the headlights did I regain my bearing. The unblinking headlights of a semi appeared, plowing through the darkness, pulling toward me so deliberately that I wondered if I'd ever reach them. Then suddenly they were upon me, and I shielded my eyes with my hand. The El Camino shook as the big rig rushed past. I watched in the rearview mirror as the red taillights got smaller and smaller, fading into nothingness like some worthless memory.

The landfill was out in the middle of fucking nowhere, a virtual lunar landscape. As I drove down the winding dirt road, it occurred to me that I might be driving to my own execution. She'd be waiting for me there. She was going to shoot me in the head and leave my body buried beneath the refuse. And nobody would come to my funeral. It was just as well.

I finally reached the bottom of the dirt road. With my high beams on I could see the vast ocean of garbage. I turned off the engine and lit a cigarette. Then I honked the horn three times and pushed open the car door. The wind was blowing all hot and tired. The moon hid behind a cloud. I stood there for a while, knowing she was perched on a hill just watching and waiting. I cleared my throat and spat on the ground. Then I started walking.

Over the next several days, I became engulfed in a whiskey-induced paranoia. I barely left the house at all. Instead, I sat in the kitchen and stared straight ahead, waiting for that silver hammer to smash the remainder of my soul into a million eulogies. Every time I heard the drone of a car's engine or saw a shadow through the drawn curtains, I figured they were coming for me, those faceless beasts that hid in the shadows, lurked in the alleys, and crawled through my brain. My sticking knife was always within reach, as was the specter of Ruth's memory. When I did leave the house—to buy booze or ramen soup—I constantly looked over my shoulder to make sure I wasn't being followed. My mind played tricks on me. I heard sirens when there were none; odd shapes floated aimlessly in the darkness...

I was certain they would come when I was sleeping. Each night I willed myself to stay awake. I removed the shades from all the ceiling lights to make my house brighter. I kept the lights on twenty-four hours a day. Some nights I would try to remember every single person I had ever met. Other nights I would count all the hairs on my arms. And when all else failed, I used a rusty old nail, stabbing myself in the stomach whenever that whore named Sleep whispered lovingly in my ear.

But one morning, after spending a sleepless night hiding in my closet with only a bottle of poison to keep me company, I decided I could take it no longer. A wild beast doesn't wait placidly in his cage while death awaits him, and neither would I.

I sat in a tire swing across the railroad tracks from Scarlett's house. Her car, an old gold Trans-Am was parked out front. The curtains were closed, but every now and then I saw her silhouette moving across the little shack. We hadn't spoken since I'd made my accusation. I'd left a couple of messages, said I wanted to trust her, but she hadn't returned the calls. I needed to know. Was she making any extravagant purchases? Snakeskin boots?

Diamond necklaces? Botox injections? And the bigger question, the thing eating up inside me: was there another man? Greed I could forgive. Infidelity? Never.

She didn't leave the house until early afternoon. It was getting hot. The sun was an orange ball of fire. You could have fried an egg on the back of my neck. Scarlett got into her car. I hid behind the tree, kept my eyes focused on her. She was wearing a summer dress, an oversized hat, and dark sunglasses. She adjusted the rearview mirror, put lipstick on. She was high fashion. I waited until she pulled away. Then I raced to my car, hit the engine and followed after her, keeping a full block distance.

For the next couple of hours, Scarlett Acres, stripper, potential blackmailer, ran mundane errands through downtown Huerfano. Grocery store, dry cleaner, hairstylist. And then she drove home. If she was in possession of my blood money, she wasn't showing signs of impulsivity. And every stripper I'd ever known was impulsive.

I parked my car and killed the engine. Grocery bags dangling from her hands, dry-cleaning flung over her shoulder, hair newly dyed, Scarlett strode through her dirt yard and into her pink house. Grabbing a pack of cigarettes and a box of Milk Duds from the dashboard, I stepped outside and returned to my watch point behind the mesquite tree. I popped a Milk Dud into my mouth and crunched down. Then I waited for something to happen.

If you've ever stalked someone—and who among us hasn't?—you begin to realize that most of the time people are boring as hell. We watch television. We eat sandwiches. Sometimes peanut butter, sometimes tuna fish. We take pisses. We take shits. Some wipe sitting, some wipe standing. We stretch. We sneeze. We pick our noses. We talk on the telephone, spreading our boredom across this great land.

Two packs of cigarettes and three boxes of candy later, the sun ducked below the desert floor, a felon on the lam. Then the moon appeared, hung-over as hell, sipping from the Pepto-Bismol sky.

Eleven o'clock and I was damn near ready to give up, feeling somewhat ashamed for suspecting my sweet Scarlett. I smoked another cigarette down to the ember and crushed it out on the bottom of my shoe. I had just started making my way to my piece-of-shit car when I heard the hum of a motor. I knelt down in the dirt. The car, a black Lincoln Continental, stopped in front of Scarlett's house. Minutes passed before the driver's-side door opened. I held my breath. He walked toward the house and pushed open the gate. I squinted. I almost didn't recognize him without his porkpie hat. His ghost walk gave him away: heel landing first, followed by the outer ridge, and a push off the toe.

He knocked on the door with his fingertips. The door opened and the light filtered over his pallid face. He said a few words and the door opened wider. He stepped inside. Then the door closed behind them, and all those ugly thoughts started crawling into my skull.

The hours slipped away incognito. And the front door remained closed. They were together. Plotting. Laughing. I rose to my feet. My legs weren't mine. I struggled to my car, dragging myself by the hair. I pulled open the driver's-side door and collapsed onto the seat. I stared at the windshield. And all I saw was darkness, darkness, darkness.

* * *

I'd always known Jack Marteau was an enabler. I'd known he was a manipulator, a liar. Under the guise of providing reassurance and fatherly advice, I'd known he only aimed to suffocate my super ego. I'd known he worshiped sin and disdained righteousness. I'd known all this. But even Lucifer has a motive for destruction. I couldn't figure out Marteau's angle. Why was he sabotaging my relationship with Scarlett? What did the devil have to gain?

CHAPTER 21

You get so lonely. You sit in the living room with the lights out, and you wait. You keep hoping you're wrong, that the girl is faithful, but you know the truth. She'd stab you in the throat and watch you spasm, the blood splattering against the dull yellow walls. And all for a buck. I don't know why I cared. We all spend our lives doing exactly what she did: imitating, acting like something we aren't, striving to become a caricature of something others want us to be. Meanwhile, when nobody is looking, we're smearing ourselves with deceit, violence, and ruthlessness and laughing all the while.

The night lasted forever. I couldn't sleep. I caught a glimpse of myself in the bathroom mirror. My hair and beard were long and unruly, my face gaunt and sunken, my eyes bloodshot and wild-looking.

The next morning several fresh and bloody tattoos had appeared on my chest and shoulders. Upside-down crosses. Words written in cursive. Complete gibberish, all of it. My body wasn't mine anymore. Neither was my mind. You lose yourself and everything makes sense…

I knew Scarlett would return. Trying to suck the remaining humanity from my intestines. She stood at the doorway wearing blue jeans and a silver halter top. She looked happy and tan and remorseless. There was a bead of sweat above her lip and the faint outline of a mustache. I'd never noticed it before. The sun was high in the sky—a belligerent motherfucker.

"I've missed you," she said, her left cheek twitching.

"The hell you have."

"Can I come in?"

"Depends. Got any whiskey?"

"It's a little early for that, don't you think, Frankie?"

"Last I checked we still lived in America."

Scarlett entered and sat down on the couch. I leaned against the wall and lit a cigarette. Now that I studied Scarlett, really studied her, I realized she didn't look a thing like my mother. Not a thing.

"You look like hell," she said.

"You're not exactly the Mona Lisa."

She chewed on her nails. Her face was too long. Her eyes were too green. "I didn't send that letter," she said. "I'd never do that to you."

"Thanks for clearing that up. Anything else?"

"I shouldn't have come," she said.

"No. You shouldn't have."

"It's just that...I just wanted to tell you..."

"Wanted to tell me what?"

Scarlett rose from the couch, walked slowly to the window, and pulled back the curtain. Then she shook her head. "Huerfano, Arizona, has to be the worst place in the entire world, don't you think, Frankie?"

I shrugged. "I don't know. I haven't done much traveling."

She turned and faced me. "I could use a drink. Will you get me something?"

"What do you want?"

"How about champagne?"

"I've got gin."

"I hate gin."

I didn't care too much. I found a glass slipper in the closet, filled it to the heel, and handed it to her. She shrugged before greedily swallowing down the booze. She wiped her face with the back of her hand and smiled meagerly. I sat on the arm of the couch, tilted the bottle into the ready position and opened my throat. My liver gagged and cursed. "You wanted to tell me something," I said. My voice was all dried up.

"Yes," she said. "I did."

"Whenever you're ready."

Scarlett wiped a strand of bleached-blonde hair out of her face. She looked at her feet and bit her lower lip. Then she laid it on me. "I'm pregnant," she said.

"Say again?"

"I took a home pregnancy test yesterday. It came back positive."

My heart jumped through my esophagus, choking me for a moment. But I acted cool. I pointed at the bottle of gin. "You sure you're supposed to be drinking this stuff?" I asked.

"My mother drank while she was pregnant, and I turned out just fine," she said.

"Matter of opinion," I mumbled.

"You don't seem very excited."

"I'm not especially. Have you figured out who the father is yet? Guess you'll have to use the white pages and start in the As."

She smiled and shook her head. "You're the father, Frankie," she said. "You're the only one."

At first I felt anger, a slow-burning rage that started in my face and traveled all the way through my body. But the anger didn't last long. Pretty soon it was replaced with resignation, then hilarity. You're the father, she'd said. It was humorous, damn it, and if you don't think so, then you don't have a funny bone in your body. A grin spread onto my face, and I started laughing, not your typical superficial laughter, but the kind of laughter that comes from deep within your belly, deep within your soul. Scarlett just sat there watching me, not sure how to respond. I was laughing and laughing and hiccupping and farting and belching and peeing and shitting. My stomach started hurting so bad that I stopped for a moment, but then I thought about everything again, and I kept right on laughing for another two or three minutes at least.

"You mind letting me in on the joke?" she finally said.

"It's just my life," I said, wiping away the tears. "I guess you had to be there."

"I don't...I don't understand."

So I showed her. I showed her what was so fucking funny. I unbuckled my belt. Yes, sir, that's what I did. I yanked my jeans down below my knees. And I pulled down my frayed boxers, the ones with horses on them...

Dad's drunk. I can hear him banging downstairs, falling over furniture, cursing. I'm lying in my bed, terrified, pretending to be asleep. He already showed Mom a thing or two. He's coming to get me next. "We've gotta kill him, Frankie, we've gotta kill him!"

Now he's standing outside my door. I can see his shadow underneath the frame. I can hear him breathing. The door opens. Light filters through the room. I don't move.

He stands there for an hour. Or maybe it just feels that way. Then I hear his footsteps marching slowly across the room, the floorboards creaking beneath his boots. He kneels next to me, smooths back my hair with his hand. He smells like whiskey and cigarettes. "It would have been better," he says in a whisper. He doesn't complete the sentence. More time passes. I'm gonna burst out screaming or laughing. "It would have been better if I'd shot your mama in the belly when you was inside."

I open my eyes. He's grinning. His face is red. He looks like the devil. He is the devil. He's holding a jackknife. It's glistening. It's the same knife he used on Mom...

Then I'm a cornered animal. I leap to my feet, start yelling, flailing around. "Ain't nobody gonna hear you, boy," he says. "We's all alone."

He's got rope too. I hadn't seen it before. I'm kicking and screaming and biting. He's too big. Six foot three. Two hundred thirty pounds. An imposing figure. He hits me with a forearm shiver. My head snaps backward. I land on the ground. He kneels down, presses the knife against my throat. "I ought to kill you right now," he says. "But that'd be letting you off too easy."

He ties my hands together. I'm not fighting anymore. I'm hanging from the rafters watching it all happen down below. He yanks my jeans down to my ankles. I know what's going to happen. I grit my teeth and close my eyes. For a few moments I don't feel anything. Then the knife is covered with blood, my blood. Some things are worse than dying...

Scarlett couldn't take her eyes off me. A fucking freak show. It was so tragic. She just stared and stared, shaking her head, mumbling inaudibly.

"So you see," I said very self-assured, "I don't think it's very likely that I'm the father of your love child. Not likely at all."

She started crying. Poor thing. You hate to be the bearer of bad news. You hate to be the destroyer of illusion.

"But you...we..."

"A fellow gets real good at compensating," I said. "First thing: make sure the lights are out. That's key. Keep your partner's hands above waist level at all times. Then, you use what you've got. A carrot stick. A dill pickle. Your fingers. You'd be surprised. Very few complaints. Many satisfied customers."

"Oh Frankie," she sobbed. "It's terrible. It's so terrible."

I pulled up my boxers and my pants. I laughed some more. It was cleansing. "I'm not a man," I said through giggles. "I'm a eunuch."

"It's okay," she said, her voice trembling. "I could still love you."

I took a couple of steps toward her. Outside the sun was waving its arms, jumping up and down, screaming. "It all makes sense now," I said.

Scarlett backed up until she couldn't back up anymore. "What makes sense, Frankie?"

I took a drag of the cigarette, letting the smoke trickle out of my nostrils. Then I willed a grin to my face. "I followed you yesterday," I said.

"What?"

"Followed you. Watched every move you made. Like that Police song."

Scarlett giggled nervously. "Now why'd you do that for?"

"See here's the thing I've learned about women. It's taken me an awful long time to reach this conclusion, but now that I know, everything makes sense."

"What? What makes sense?"

"Every woman, old or young, skinny or fat, acne-scarred or not, is a whore. They fuck and betray, fuck and betray. They suck the life out of your veins when you're sleeping and gnaw on your soul when you're drunk."

"That's a terrible thing to say."

"I watched you. And I saw him. Saw him enter your house. Saw the front door close. And stay closed."

The color washed away from her face, but she recovered nicely. "You're mistaken, Frankie. Nobody entered my house last night."

"So you're gonna keep playing that game, huh? Like when I saw the two of you outside the diner? It was just my imagination. I'm fucking delusional, is that it?"

"That's not what I said."

"He's so fucking convincing, isn't he? So smooth. He takes the most ridiculous notions and makes them seem reasonable. Stronger people would laugh in his face. But we're weak, you and I. He tells us what we want to hear. And we do what he tells us."

"I...I thought you would leave me, Frankie. I can't stay in this town another day. Can't you see that I'm dying? Can't you see that I'm withering away?"

I took another step forward. "You've got the devil's child growing in your belly."

Scarlett shook her head. "Frankie..."

I touched her shoulder gently, the way a doctor might comfort a cancer patient. "It's not your fault," I said. "None of it. God made you this way. He made you spiteful, cold, and mean. And there wasn't a thing you could do about it."

Scarlett looked at me with resignation in her eyes, and I slapped her. She bowed her head in shame. I placed my hand under her chin, lifted up her head. Then I reached back and swung as hard as I could, connecting with her cheekbone. She crumpled to the floor like a dress falling from a hanger. I pulled her back up. I gave her a jab with the left, a hook with the right. Her head swung back and forth like a spastic pendulum. I kept after her, one fist, then the other, preventing her from falling. And then I stopped punching and she collapsed to the floor, a heap of heartache. She was still breathing, but her face was all disfigured. Blood was spilling from her nose and her left eye was swollen shut. She was moaning, trying to speak, poor thing. I knelt beside her, kissed her busted nose, tasted the blood. "I'm sorry," I said. "Goddamn it, I'm sorry."

I tried pulling her to her feet. Her body wasn't working. She kept losing her balance. I bent down and grabbed a hold of her hair, which was tied back in a horsetail. I dragged her across the living room. Her mouth opened but nothing came out except for babbles and screeches.

I stopped in front of the basement staircase, all eleven cement steps. "I'm gonna help you to your feet," I said. "Everything's gonna be all right." I reached beneath her arms and pulled her to a standing position. As I stood there holding her tight, I might have felt a tinge of happiness. But happiness is fleeting. I knew it'd never last. I released my grip. She started wobbling and staggering. She had no equilibrium, you see. I waited until she was centered with the staircase and then let 'er rip with a round-house right. She toppled backward down the concrete stairs, a bleach-blonde rag doll nobody wanted anymore.

CHAPTER 22

That night I couldn't sleep. I just lay in bed, staring at the ceiling, thinking torturous thoughts. I tried pushing them from my consciousness, but they kept reappearing, quick jabs to the inside of my skull. I can't even articulate what the content of the thoughts were; they were blurry and formless. I reached over to the nightstand and pulled out a bent cigarette from my pack and lit it. I closed my eyes and inhaled. I touched my fingers to my right biceps, felt the scar of her name. I grinned. I still hadn't rid myself of her. Every goddamn time I took off my shirt that fucking tattoo would be there to remind me. Unless...

Looking back on it now, it seems a little crazy, but at the time there didn't seem to be another choice. I crushed out my cigarette on the windowsill and rolled out of bed. I went into the kitchen and poured myself a nice tall glass of whiskey and chased it down with some rum, then chased that down with some vodka, then chased that down with...well, you get the point. By the time I was done prepping myself for the operation, I was so plastered I couldn't have told my ass from a hole in my story. I somersaulted my way back into the bedroom and located my old workbag underneath a heap of dirty clothes. I pulled a knife out of the bag—the same one I once used for sticking cattle—and began sharpening it. I must have looked like a goddamn virtuoso violinist performing in the moonlight. After about twenty minutes I gave the knife a quick test on my finger. It was plenty sharp. I poured some vodka onto my arm to sterilize the tattoo, then took another gulp to sterilize my nerves.

Even considering how drunk I was, the operation hurt plenty, believe me. It wasn't a tiny tattoo, and I had to cut pretty deep to remove it. A few times the pain was so intense that I nearly gave up, but then I remembered her evil face and pressed forward.

When the operation was complete, I wiped the blood off the table and wrapped a towel around the wound before dragging my depleted body to the bed and closing my eyes. I could smell the memory of her on the pillow, so I cursed and threw it on the ground. Eventually I fell asleep, but I woke up every half hour screaming bloody murder.

Two thirty-six and I heard a rattling at my front door. I looked up, eyes all glazed with ethanol. My sanity had been bound and gagged. Thousands of army ants were marching into my house dragging another tattered envelope, the latest installment of "Frankie Avicious: Damned to Hell." With piercing screams they scurried toward me, ready to devour my wounded flesh. Letting loose a scream of my own, I leapt to the floor and grabbed the envelope from their masses. A dozen or more gluttonous ants crawled on my arm, chomping at my skin.

With great hysterics, I tore open the envelope. Inside was a photograph, all tattered and faded. I was fifteen years old. I was standing outside in a vast desert wilderness. Not far from Huerfano. The sun was setting behind me. I was naked, crouching like a savage. The area around my groin had not yet healed and was all swollen and bloody. My chest was also covered in blood. I was grinning crazily. My arms were raised in the manner of a victorious Indian chief. And clenched between my hands was what appeared to be a gruesome Halloween mask or a macabre sculpture of a human head. But I knew better. She'd taken the photograph so we'd have a memento, a reminder that after all the meanness and cruelty he'd showed us through the years, we'd taken mighty good care of that bastard.

And on the back of the photograph were two words: *Balance owed.* I crumpled the photograph in my hand and cursed. You hate to kill the wrong person. It happens, but you hate it when it does.

Glancing back down at the floor, I noticed the ants were continuing to multiply. There must have been a hundred thousand or more, creating the odd illusion that the floor itself was in motion. Spine tightening with panic, I raced to the kitchen and kicked open the sink cabinet. Knocking over detergents and rat poisons and industrial-strength cleaners, I located a bottle of lighter fluid. I raced back to the living room where the ants had begun eating through the floorboards and rugs. I squeezed the lighter fluid, drenching all those predatory insects as they shrieked with primordial rage. Creeping closer to the door, I pulled out a box of matches. I lit one. My hands were shaking badly. I took a deep breath. Then I threw that match down and watched hell swallow everything in its path.

I kicked the front door open and tumbled outside onto

the dirt, watching as the rickety old house became engulfed in fire, the tall flames rising to the bitumen sky. Burn, ants, burn! Then all the people emerged from their homes, the same curious bystanders who watch in disguised glee every time there is a car wreck on the highway or a shooting outside a nightclub, milling around the yard murmuring to each other, shaking their heads, and pointing at poor little me.

A few of these monsters caused more chaos by crawling all over my car, busting windshields and slashing tires. I charged after them, thumping my chest, but they just kept right on vandalizing and tormenting, gleeful shouts mixing with the hot-rod flames.

Leaving my smoldering skin by the side of the road, I ran through the streets of Huerfano, my bones clattering against the asphalt. Every few seconds I glanced over my shoulder waiting for the guillotine to drop.

I was desperate. I needed to get the rest of the money. Otherwise I was a dead man. I was sure of it. The banks were all closed. And the ATMs were out of business. I saw an old woman walking with a cane. Her hair was blue and she was wearing Ray Charles sunglasses. She was holding a flower purse. I asked her for the time, then shoved her to the ground. She fractured her hip. I grabbed her purse. As I fled the scene, I rifled through the contents. Driver's license, American Express card, dirty handkerchief, photo of her dead husband, photo of her ugly grandchildren, pack of gum. Twelve dollars in cash. I did some quick math. At this pace I'd have to mug more than three hundred grandmas. That might take me all night.

Other options. My mother-in-law would help me out. Of course she would. She was family. She might have some hooker money lying around. I didn't know why I hadn't thought of her earlier. With renewed vigor, I scurried through the streets, crawled over cars, and swung around lampposts. I borrowed a teenager's skateboard and rolled down the avenue until I came to her house. When I reached her front door, my shirt was torn and the moon was cracked.

All the curtains were shut, but the lights were on. I pounded on the door with my fist. My legs were all rubbery and I was having a hard time standing. I waited a minute or more. Nobody answered. With adrenaline and blood dribbling from my nostrils, I took a few steps back, raced forward, and rammed into the door. The goddamn thing didn't budge, and I dislocated my shoulder. Next I tried the doorknob. It was unlocked.

I stepped inside. The television was on. An infomercial was playing. A fat bald man was selling something called a Flowbee: a vacuum cleaner that apparently gave haircuts. Nobody was watching. I turned it off. "Marilyn?" I called out. "Fred? Are you there?" No answer.

I went into the bedroom. The bed was unmade. Incense was burning. Fred's postal bag was on the floor, mail undelivered. Yesterday's newspaper lay on a wicker chair. I walked to the far side of the room and came to a bureau. Sticking a cigarette into the corner of my mouth, I started rifling through the drawers, looking for jewelry or money or gold. I found dental floss and bug spray and duct tape.

I used the incense to light my cigarette. Then I went to the kitchen. Dishes were piled in the sink and the water was running. I opened the fridge. There was a three-pack of Schlitz. Out of consideration, I only drank two of them. But then I was still thirsty, so I downed the third one too.

I had to take a piss. I lumbered down the hallway toward the bathroom. The door was closed. There was blood on the doorknob. I should have walked away. I was curious. I opened the door. I vomited on my shoes. The floors and walls were covered with blood. Marilyn Cook was covered with piss and blood. Her head was in the toilet. And the seat was up.

Feeling more than a little bit woozy, I stumbled through the house and tumbled out the front door. I was shocked to come face-to-face with my old buddy Simon Harris.

"Frankie," he said. "What the heck are you doing here?"

"I only came here for money," I said. "You can't blame me..."

I pushed my way past him, put my head down and ran blindly through the midnight-darkened streets of a town heavily medicated and on life support.

On the east side of the highway—away from Huerfano proper—was a short strip of motels, gas stations, and diners. The Paradise was one of those motels. Surrounded by a dried-up swimming pool, an empty parking lot, and ghosts of vacations past, it was just biding its time, waiting for the inevitable. I got a room there.

Inside everything was dingy. Paint was peeling from the ceiling. The rug had strange-looking stains on it. The television was broken and so was the chair. In the corner of the room, a swamp cooler was rumbling. I took off my shirt and stood in front of the cooler for a few minutes.

Then I lay down and stared at the ceiling.

At midnight the phone started ringing. It rang and rang and rang, twenty times at least, then suddenly stopped. I exhaled. But then, not a minute later, the tortuous ringing started again. I covered my ears with my hands and gritted my teeth. It was getting to be too much to take. In desperation, I yanked the cord out of the wall. I tried to sleep, all curled up in the corner of the room. But there was no relief. Just nightmares and dry heaves.

And then my eyes flew open and I saw the silhouette of a man in the doorway, his shadow stretching within inches of my cowardly body. The door slammed shut. He took a couple of steps forward. He walked with a limp. Step, drag. Step, drag. I cowered in the corner, no gun, no knife, no chance. He stood over me. Then he turned on the dresser lamp and I saw his face, all angry and monstrous and deformed. I'd seen him before. At the cemetery. Hiding behind the tree. Our eyes met and he bared his teeth.

"I ought to kill you," he said in a boy's voice. "The world would be a better place."

"Not for me it wouldn't."

He sneered. "You owe me some money. Four thousand and change." His eyes were different colors. One brown. One gray.

"I gave you all I have," I said.

"You're a fucking liar!" he shouted. Then he smiled. "Won't it be fun when the whole world finds out about your perversions? When the whole world learns you're a murderer?"

His face was covered with bitterness and rage. I rose from the floor. I lit a cigarette and sucked down some smoke, keeping it inside my lungs as long as possible before spitting it toward the ceiling. I paced around the room, my head spinning, my heart flopping like a carp.

"Who are you?" I said. "Where'd you get the picture?"

"I'm just a guy looking for a quick buck."

"I know you from somewhere."

"The cemetery."

"No. Before that. From a long time ago."

He smiled. "Your mind is playing tricks on you."

"The picture you have," I said. "It means nothing. I was just posing. Mother pulled the trigger. And she confessed to the crime. I'm sure you read about it in the newspapers. You think they'd charge me now? Based on that photo? You're crazy."

"You want to take that chance?" he said.

"Maybe I do."

He shook his head ruefully. "And what about the rest of it?" he said. "Forget the murder. Hell, that's a crime you could have been proud of. What about the rest of it?"

"I don't know what you're talking about."

He cleared his throat. "The fact that you were fucking your mother, Frankie. It doesn't get any seamier than that, does it?"

My stomach tightened. I felt like I was going to be sick. "I never did that," I said. "That was just a rumor, started by nasty people."

He chuckled. "Aw, who are you kidding? Let's face the facts. You got her pregnant."

"No, I...I..."

"And when there's incest, there's an increased likelyhood of birth defects, an increased likelihood of micro-cephaly, of spina bifida, of encephalocele, of Down syn-drome, of dwarfism, of club foot…"

Fear slammed into my rib cage. I tried speaking. My jaw was too heavy. "You're not…you're not…"

"If you can look past the deformities and defects, if you can peer past the repulsive nature of my appearance, you'll see the truth."

I staggered backward, my organs all collapsing into each other. "No," I said. "It can't be. She said—"

"That she was going to have an abortion. But she couldn't. She just couldn't. Then she would have had nothing left. She named me after you. Frankie Junior. I was conceived in love."

But his mismatched eyes were full of hatred. What had Mother told him? What lies had she nourished him with?

"I need an operation," he said. "My heart, can you believe it? All of this repulsiveness and it's my heart that's gonna do me in. The insurance won't cover all the costs. I'm not a bad person. What I am I supposed to do? Just wither away? Forget it, Jake, it's Chinatown."

"Fuck you!" I shouted. "You're not my son! You're a freak, a fucking freak!"

Then everything was a blur. He came charging at me, screeching like a hawk, pile-driving me onto the ground. With fury spilling from the corners of his mouth, he head-butted me, cracking my forehead open. Then he pressed his forearm against the bottom of my chin and pinned my body down with his legs. I was paralyzed.

"Pray to God for your life."

I shook my head. "He won't listen to me."

He lurched forward. I felt a sharp pain in my gut, right

above my belt. I gasped and groaned. I was ready to call it a night. He rolled off me and rose to his feet. Then he stood over me, his misshapen face full of shock, a bloody jackknife dangling from his hand. "I didn't mean to…"

I closed my eyes and clenched my jaw. I could feel my life, all warm and sticky, drizzling across my skin.

CHAPTER 23

I heard voices. Faraway voices like I was still dreaming. I opened my eyes. They stung. Everything was blurry and white. White walls. White ceilings. White uniforms. I blinked a few times. A woman's face came into focus. She was a nurse. She was holding a plastic bag filled with my piss.

"Is this heaven?" I said, my mouth all full of cotton balls.

"St. Luke's Hospital."

"I don't have insurance," I said. "And I'm not Catholic. Although I do like Catholic schoolgirls. Those plaid skirts."

She smiled, but it wasn't a sweet or comforting smile. "You don't need insurance, Mr. Avicious."

"And it's about time," I said. "You know, I've been preaching about universal health care for years."

"You," she said, sticking an IV in my arm, "are lucky to be alive."

"Luck's got nothing to do with it."

"You lost a lot of blood. Another ten minutes and it would have been too late."

I tried sitting up, but it was no good. The pain was too much. "Did they catch him?" I said.

She stuck some pink pills in my mouth and jammed my jaw shut. "Catch who?"

"The man who stabbed me. I can give you a description. He's got an uncanny resemblance to a geriatric asshole."

The nurse turned me over and administered an enema. I crapped all over her starched outfit. "Now you just take it easy and don't worry about any geriatric assholes," she said. "And let me know if there's anything I can do to make you a little more comfortable."

She wiped off her uniform with a wet paper towel and walked across the room, her white sneakers squeaking on the linoleum floor. The door creaked open.

And that's when I saw the two police officers standing guard outside my room, hands within a whisker of their weapons.

Detective Johnson showed up later that evening. His eyes were tired and bloodshot, and he was in bad need of a shave. He stood over my hospital bed and shook his head slowly. "It's all over, Frankie," he said. "We've got a witness. You got sloppy."

"Witness?"

"Simon Harris. He saw you leaving Marilyn Cook's house. Mumbling how it wasn't your fault. Another corpse, Frankie. They're piling up, aren't they?"

"No," I said. "You've got it all wrong. I didn't kill Marilyn. Fred. He...he..."

"Stop it, Frankie. Fred's alibi is airtight. He was with Janet Reno, the local hooker."

"You gonna take some whore's word over mine?"

"You're going to hell for this one, Frankie. You bashed her fucking brains in. Stuck her in the toilet. You sick fuck. Even if we can't get you for the others, this one's a slam dunk. Witness. Fingerprints. Motive."

"Motive?"

"It's always about the money, isn't it, Frankie? Marilyn was set to receive a good portion of her ex-husband's inheritance. He apparently still cared for the old hag. But with her and Ruth out of the way..."

I shook my head and rubbed my cheek. "That's crazy. You've got it all wrong."

"Innocent lives, Frankie. Squashed like bugs. And for what? An inheritance you'll never collect. A payoff that will cost you your life."

I grinned. "Now, now, Detective. You've got me figured all wrong. I'm a swell guy, really I am. I wouldn't kill anybody, I'm too goddamn gentle. Always have been. But maybe I should speak to a lawyer. Just in case, you know?"

Johnson nodded solemnly. "I think that's a mighty good idea, Frankie."

They discharged me on a Thursday and transferred me to the county jail. The holding cell was typical. In one corner there was a cot with nightmares rotting beneath the sheets. In the other corner there was a toilet with crap rotting in the water. A light hung from the ceiling. I couldn't see outside, but I could look out into the corridor and see the facades of other cells where tattooed arms hung outside the bars. Lunatic screams echoed against the walls.

I spent seven weeks in holding, taking a few field trips to the courthouse for preliminary hearings and pretrial motions. I was permitted out of my cell twice a day. Once to shower. I had eight minutes inside a converted phone booth. I was expected to wash all parts of my body and rinse my hair. There were four guards with guns and billy clubs to make sure. I kid you not. The other time was to exercise. The exercise area was a small blacktop sur-rounded by concrete walls that rose thirty feet above the ground. The roof was made of metal beams, covered by wire mesh. There was a walking track and a bench press with weights welded on it. I would have tried to use it, but it looked pretty damn heavy. Instead I just sat on the ground and counted my blessings. I usually made it to zero.

I tried to sleep as much as possible. At first, I dreamt of the outside world. The sun, the sky, the trees. My mother. My childhood. But eventually those images dissolved and I began to dream only of life in my cell. Inmates. Metal bars. Shadows. It was as if my brain had finally realized that my body was imprisoned. I was surrounded by silence. I used to watch as spiders crawled from beneath my bed and made their way under the cell door. And I envied those goddamn spiders, hell yes I did. My spirit was gradually being whittled down to nothing. Boredom and loneliness interrupted every so often by fits of violence. Not only was I was being treated as if I were unfit for life, I was being treated as if I were unfit for death.

So eventually I lost hope. I tried hanging myself with my bedsheet. The sheet was too long. A guard got wind of my attempt. "Next time you try killing yourself, you might want to think about succeeding," he told me. Sound advice.

* * *

Other than my lawyer, I hadn't had a single visitor in my time at the D-Unit. So I was surprised when, shortly after my breakfast of peppered vulture crap, my cell door opened and there stood an old man in a crazy priest getup. He had closely sheared gray hair, a stout ruddy face, and accusing blue eyes. Stuck beneath his arm was a thick leather book—*The Complete Idiot's Guide to Avoiding Hell.*

He took a couple of cautious steps forward and the door shut behind him. Without waiting for introductions, I pulled down my pants and sat down on the pot to take a piss. The chaplain looked away, adjusting his crazy getup. "My name is Father Donnelly," he said, "and I'm here to help."

"Don't need it," I said. "Thanks anyway."

He cleared his throat. "I don't pretend to know the pain you're feeling."

"I could fill you in pretty quickly."

"I understand you tried taking your own life."

I finished my business and wiped off my exposed urethra. "Yeah, well. Figured I've done enough damage on Earth. Decided to try my luck down below."

Donnelly walked slowly across the cell and placed his hand on my shoulder. "Then you haven't accepted Jesus?"

"Not the one you're thinking about. But there is this fellow named Jesus that I used to work with. Jesus Rodriquez. I accepted him just fine. Even lent him twenty bucks once. Never did pay me back…"

"Eternal life is still within your grasp," he said.

"Eternal life? Fuck, I just tried killing myself. Everlasting life is the last thing I want."

The chaplain eyed me warily. "Those who believe that Christ was the Messiah, the Son of God, will receive a place in heaven."

I laughed. "I know the deal. I've read the Bible. But let me ask you something. Don't you think Christ is just a tad bit egomaniacal?"

"Egomaniacal?"

"Yeah. You know. Starved for adoration. Only providing eternal bliss to those who'll suck his little carpenter dick."

Donnelly's face reddened. "That's blasphemous, Mr. Avicious."

"I'm sorry," I said. "Sometimes my tongue works quicker than my brain. Honestly though. I've tried believing. Really, I have. How do you do it? I mean, you seem like an intelligent man. How do you go about believing in a virgin birth, water into wine, bodily resurrection, and the rest of that crap? It seems pretty fantastical, if you ask me."

He responded quickly, instinctively. "All you have to do is look around. His fingerprints are everywhere."

I nodded my head thoughtfully. "Famine, genocide, and war. Yeah, I see what you mean."

"No, those are the fingerprints of man. Sunsets, mountaintops, and human kindness. That's what originates from God."

"You're good," I said. "You're very good. I can see why you became a man of God. You must think about this crap all the time. But I'm still worried. What if I just can't bring myself to believe? What if I try and try and try to no avail? What if I listen to the preachers and read the

Bible and go to church and decide it's a bunch of hypocritical crap? What then? The highway to hell? The fiery furnace?"

"It's not my job to judge," he said. "Only the Father can save souls."

"Oh, to hell with that. You're judging all the time. You see your belief system as the right one. Means all the others must be wrong."

"I believe there are many paths to God."

"And just as many to hell," I said, my voice rising. "I know what you really think: Angels and swans and Enya for all the good little Christian boys and girls. Flesh burning and ravens plucking eyes from the Muslims and Hindus and Buddhists and atheists. And me. That's what you think."

The chaplain gazed at me for a few moments, his left cheek twitching. Then his purple lips spread into a grin, and he chuckled. "She told me you were irreverent. Appropriate description, I should say."

"She? She who?"

"Why your mother, of course."

My heart dropped into my shoes. My hands started shaking like a leaf with Parkinson's disease. My throat got as dry and tight as a frigid virgin in bed with a balding insurance salesman. "My mother?" I croaked.

"Lovely woman," the chaplain said. "I counseled her when she was in prison. We made some real progress together."

"I heard she was dead."

"No, she's very much alive," he said. "She was recently granted parole. Just in time for your sentencing. Not that she would have been able to see you. Part of the agreement with the parole board is that she has no contact with you. Such a shame. She loves you deeply."

I paced across the cell, hands behind my head, ugly thoughts weighing down my brain. "I want to see her," I said.

"That's why I'm here."

"I thought you wanted me to find religion."

He cleared his throat and grinned bitterly. "Do you want to know the truth, Frankie?"

"Not particularly."

"The truth is that I'm a fraud, a wolf in sheep's clothing. Don't get me wrong. Once upon a time I used to believe. God works in mysterious ways and so on. But your mother...she changed all that. She's a witch, Frankie, and she put a spell on me."

The cell door crashed open and a pair of faceless prison guards entered. "Time's up," the shorter one said.

"Is he saved?" the taller one said.

Father Donnelly turned toward the guards and nodded. "Would you mind if the prisoner and I knelt down for a short prayer?"

There was a moment's hesitation. Then the short one said, "Go ahead. But make it quick."

Father Donnelly knelt down on the cold floor and motioned for me to sit next to him. I did. Our backs were to the guards. He grasped my hand and squeezed it. His skin was cold and damp. In a voice only loud enough for me to hear, he said, "I would do anything for your mother." He placed the leather-bound Bible in my hands and looked straight into my eyes. "There's a black trash can...outside...in the exercise yard...behind the weight set...beneath it there's a gun...use it...save yourself...save your mother…may Christ have mercy on your soul. May Christ have mercy on my soul."

He rose to his feet, eyes fixated on a point above my head. Then the guards escorted him out, and the cell door slammed shut, the sound echoing through the corridor.

The night lasted a decade. I lay in bed and chewed the skin off my hands. I'd long since convinced myself that she was dead. As soon as they'd cut off her pretty hair, dressed her in orange, and stuck her in that prison cell, I couldn't conceive of her still breathing and living. I'd never visited her. I'd never written to her. Tried not to think about her. And now she'd come back from the dead. Giving our memento to a freak. Conning a priest. Helping me escape. My soul had already been devoured. She was feeding on the crumbs.

CHAPTER 24

The sun: brutal and callous, swathed in desert dust. The inmates: a mass of evil, slithering around the asphalt circle. The guards: baby-faced Hitler youth, eyes shifting, ready to shatter skulls. I walked slowly around the exercise circle, head down, trying to make myself invisible. Here I wasn't a murderer, rapist, or drug dealer. I was just another prisoner, number six-five-five-three-two-one stitched across my chest.

Killer Joe was on the bench press, heaving up six plates like they were powdered donuts. "Motherfucker," he yelled. "It feels so goddamn good."

The trash can with my golden ticket was about three feet from the bench. A bald man with tree-trunk arms and a handlebar mustache was leaning against it, sucking a cigarette, shielding his eyes from the sun. I stood next to him and winked. "Pardon me," I said, "but you wouldn't happen to have any Jane Austen novels I might borrow? I'm especially partial to *Sense and Sensibility*. See, I identify with Marianne Dashwood."

He looked at me and said, "What the fuck?" I had no patience for Jane Austen haters. I kneed him in the groin. He collapsed like a Chinaman after eighteen tumblers of vermouth. Within seconds, one of his buddies appeared, arms covered with tattoos of swastikas and machine guns and skulls and tulips. He wasn't so tough. He broke my nose and my jaw, then ripped out my kidney and donated it to his ailing uncle Stan in Tuscaloosa. It wasn't long before the blacks and Latinos and skinheads got into the act, fists flying, throats getting cut, blood splattering on the asphalt. A good old-fashioned riot.

The guards stood by and watched, waiting for the inmates to kill themselves off. Me, I dodged through the mayhem, blood trickling from my mouth, carousel music blasting in my head. I returned to the trash can and gave it a Bruce Lee kick to the side, but it was chained to the fence and didn't budge. Sliding to my knees, I pried the can upward with my left hand and snatched the silver Springfield Armory semiautomatic pistol with my right.

When I looked up, there was a red-faced guard with a billy club in one hand and a gun in the other. He hesitated, and I fired two shots into his stomach, paralyzing him. He mumbled something about a mistress in Phoenix before collapsing to the ground. I rose to my feet and started pumping my legs and arms, but I couldn't tell if I was actually moving. As the strange carnival continued around me, I came face-to-face with another guard, his face painted like a clown. His gun was eighteen inches from my chest. He squeezed the trigger, and there was a loud explosion. I fell flat on my back, and I thought I was a corpse for sure. The red sun appeared, burning my retinas, and the hellish silhouette of the guard rose over me. With Satan's help, I raised my gun and pointed it at his face. I fired and a black hole appeared where his right eye used to be. He stomped his foot in frustration.

I pulled myself up to a kneeling position, breathing heavily and spitting more blood. I'd been shot just below the collarbone. I wanted to give up, but then I was back on my feet, running again. Figures were hurtling at me—guards, inmates—and shots were being fired from all directions. I got hit in the back of the leg, but the adrenaline healed me, and I didn't stay on the ground for long.

Then there were deafening sounds, and I looked up, startled, and saw a man with a shaved head and army fatigues, firing a sub-machine gun. It took me a moment to realize it was Father Donnelly. He was running beside me, pausing every so often to fire at the sharpshooters in the towers. "Go to the gate!" he shouted. "It'll open!"

My body was in shock. I was running with my head down, watching out of the corner of my eye as bodies continued to fall. You gotta get there, I told myself, but when I reached the fence, the gate was closed. A uniformed man with a pencil-thin mustache appeared, and he was pointing a Winchester rifle at my poor head. A shot echoed. The guard tumbled backward, a pool of blood appearing instantaneously. I looked back and saw Donnelly standing upright with his gun at his side. He did the sign of the cross before vanishing like a specter, leaving confetti in his wake. Then the gate opened, slowly, menacingly, and I stumbled out of the prison grounds, a free man.

A gold Pontiac Sunbird was parked just outside the gates, engine humming. The rear door was open, and I dove in. As I slammed the door shut, the car lurched forward, and a husky woman's voice told me to lie on the floor so I wouldn't be seen.

Cigarette smoke and Arizona heat filled the car. Except

for the steady drone of the engine, the world was silent. From the floor of the car I could see the edges of the landscape, stark and unchanging. Orange sunlight splintered through the windows, and strange shadows danced on the ceiling. After five or ten minutes of driving, the car made a sharp left, kicking up red dust. We drove down a gravel path and into a dirt valley. The car jerked to a stop and everything was still. I sat up, my lungs filling up with dread, making it hard to breathe. The driver turned around, a savage grin on her face.

Time hadn't done her any favors. She was a wreck of a human being. Her eyes were bloodshot and mean, and her mouth was full of rotting teeth. Her hair was black and white and brittle. It was combed straight back, revealing a familiar scar: *Slut.* I tried speaking, but at first there were just squeaks and coughs. Finally I managed to sputter her name. Doris. She grunted bemusedly. Then she leaned toward me so I could smell her breath, all soggy with cigarettes and bologna. "Don't look so revolted," she said in a raspy voice. "What say you give your mother a little kiss for old time's sake?"

I shook my head and vomited on the seat. She slapped her thigh and laughed. But there were tears welling in her eyes. "You never visited me, Frankie," she said. "It was so lonely and terrible in there, and you never visited me."

"I couldn't. I couldn't."

"After all I did for you? Little fucker." She laughed a short hysterical laugh and her face brightened. "But I forgive you, Frankie. Besides. You've got the rest of your miserable life to make up for it."

* * *

The hideaway was a small adobe building with a sun-bleached painting of Jesus covering the front wall. Next to the building was a wooden shed, large enough to conceal the car. The sun beat down on the Sonora landscape. I had a sudden vision of burning to death and getting my flesh picked apart by vultures. You don't choose your thoughts, your thoughts choose you.

Inside the adobe building everything was bare, save for some empty beer cans and a broken bottle of tequila. Lizards scurried across the floor. I slumped down against a wall.

Mother looked at my orange jumpsuit, the right sleeve soaked through with blood. "You've been injured, darling."

"Yeah? I didn't notice."

"Did you get shot?"

"Nah. Cut myself shaving."

She shook her head. "Take off your shirt."

"Ever the romantic, Doris."

"I can get you fixed, Frankie. I learned a lot in prison. My cell mate was a nurse."

I grunted. "My cell mate was a child molester. Doesn't mean I should go around fondling little boys."

Mother narrowed her eyes. "Take off your shirt, Frankie."

I was tired of arguing. I unbuttoned my shirt. Mother eyed me like a dog eyeing a bone. Then she walked across the room and opened a closet door. She came out with a first-aid kit and a fresh bottle of tequila. "Drink some of this and then lie down," she said.

"Sure, Doris, sure."

I strangled the bottle by the neck and drained the life

out of it. My eyes rolled into the back of my head, and I felt the sudden urge to tap-dance in a minstrel show. I resisted. "Are you ready, Frankie?" she asked, her black eyes like pieces of coal sunken in a mound of dough. "This might hurt a bit."

"Yeah, sure," I said. "What are you going to do? A little gauze perhaps? Antibiotic cream?"

She sneered and pulled out a scalpel. I screamed.

CHAPTER 25

"Gotta get that bullet out," Mother whispered. "Otherwise, you've got no chance." She sliced and diced like a Benihana chef. The overwhelming shock prevented me from feeling any pain. After an hour or two, she managed to remove the bullet along with a quarter pound of flesh and several strange-looking muscles. Satisfied, she placed the bullet on the windowsill and licked her hands like a mutant feline. Me, I closed my eyes and fell right asleep. I slept like a baby: I woke up every couple of hours screaming and crying. My dreams were filled with battlefield carnage: young privates being blown to kingdom come.

When I woke up, the war was still raging and my mother was standing over me, dust rising in the light behind her. "You're so beautiful when you sleep," she said.

"Got a good makeup artist."

"You must be hungry," she said. "Escaping from prison and all."

"Thirsty, actually."

"How about some water?"

"Are you fucking kidding me?"

She shrugged and opened a cooler. She handed me a can of '78 Schlitz. I cracked open the beer and poured it down my throat. Mother sat down next to me and stroked my greasy hair. "I've thought about this day for such a long time," she said.

"And is it everything you imagined it to be?"

"Oh darling..."

I grunted and gargled down some more beer. "Tell me about the priest. Donnelly. How'd you get him to help me? Suck his dick?"

She frowned. "That's crude, Frankie."

"Well?"

"He'd lost his faith in God. I saw an opportunity. I took it. You're not showing much gratitude."

I finished my beer and crushed it with my foot. "I'm not in the mood for thankfulness. The priest isn't your only victim I've encountered. Had a nice little chat with your son. Our son."

Mother's eyes narrowed, and her cheek twitched. "What are you talking about?"

I tried spitting on the ground, but it landed on my foot. "What am I talking about? Frankie Junior. Lovely child. Blessed with a dozen or so birth defects. Somehow he managed to obtain a certain photograph, a memento of our crowning achievement. Can't imagine who gave him that. Son-of-a-bitch extorted my life savings."

Mother rose to her feet and wrung her hands, a constipated expression on her bitch face. I wanted so badly to slap her, to push her around, to make her scream, to make her bleed.

"I...I didn't want you to know about him. He was an orphan. I barely knew him myself. He'd visit me from time to time. He wanted to understand. I tried explaining. I told him the truth. He didn't believe me. I gave him the picture. I wasn't thinking. I never thought he'd use it against you."

I rested my head against the wall and closed my eyes. "Fuck it. It doesn't matter anymore. It's water under the bridge. Water filled with pathogens and industrial waste, but water under the bridge nonetheless."

I stayed awake for the rest of the night, the minutes slipping by in slow motion. Through the window I could see the desert sky filled with dead stars and an assassin moon. I was drifting down, down, down.

At one point during the night, a helicopter starting buzzing overhead. The trailer filled up with light, and dust swirled through the broken windows. Mother sat up, eyes shining like a cat. But soon the darkness returned and the sound of the chopper became fainter and fainter. "They missed us," Mother said. "They never knew we were here."

I wiped the sweat from my forehead and stared at my arm, all withered with gangrene. This is going to end badly, I thought. This is going to end very badly.

We left early that morning, as the sun peered over the desert floor. We drove east on Highway 8 along the banks of the dehydrated Gila River. The land was so barren and bleak that I kept forgetting I was alive. We passed a few ranching towns with names like Tacna, Aztec, and Sentinel, but otherwise the desert was comatose. The air-conditioning in the Sunbird was broken, so we had both windows open, and it was hard to make conversation. That was fine by me.

We stopped in a town called Gila Bend. Mom spotted a beauty salon on West Pima Street. She went inside and bought a scissor and some blond hair dye. Then she cut and dyed my hair in the restroom of a Sinclair station. I looked like a new man. A blond bombshell.

We were both mighty hungry, but I was worried about being seen in public. Mom told me not to sweat it. "Nobody's gonna recognize you, not with that blond hair. Besides. You can't live your life in fear. *Carpe diem.*"

I wanted pizza and Mom wanted Chinese, so we settled on Mexican. We found a little hole-in-the-wall called Sofia's, and I figured it must be good because they were passing out green cards at the door.

I didn't have much of an appetite. I ordered *carne asada*, a breakfast burrito, and an enchilada smothered in green chili. Mom got a salad. Through most of dinner we ate in silence, but every so often she would gaze up at me, her mouth curled up in a slight grin, her green eyes too jolly for the circumstances. Being in a cantankerous mood, I decided to set her straight on a few things. "Considering that from now on we're going to be stuck to each other like yellow on piss, I think it's important we be clear on who wears the pants in this here family. Let me start, Doris, with my own qualifications." In between bites of food, I proceeded to spit out detailed summation of my recent violent rampage. I told her about Dick Richardson and José Gutierrez and Ponso Arguello and Ruth Avicious and Scarlett Acres. I tried to be as explicit as possible when discussing the suffering each victim endured. "I'm not a masochist and I'm not a braggart, Doris. I only want you to understand that at no point in our road trip will I hesitate to stick a gun down your throat if you so much as contemplate betraying me."

Feeling satisfied with my verbal ejaculation, I stuffed

the last piece of enchilada in my mouth and released a loud belch. Mother just stared at me, rage filling her pupils. She took a bite of her dinner salad, chewing slowly. Then she dropped her fork to her plate, reached across the table and slapped me so hard I felt my brain bounce. "Don't ever talk to your mother that way," she said. "I didn't raise a hoodlum." Then her face softened and she cocked a painted eyebrow. "Besides, Frankie. I'm not afraid of dying. Dying is the easy part."

We drove like sons-of-bitches the next couple of days, finishing off Arizona and New Mexico with a kick to the temple before entering the scarred badlands of West Texas. We could have gotten farther, but Mother insisted on stopping at every goddamn roadside attraction: a trading post called "The Thing," with its mysterious mummified corpse; the OK Corral in Tombstone; the Queen Mine in Bisbee; the endless underground caves of the Carlsbad Caverns. We were risking being spotted, but it was worth it. She was trying to make up for my dysfunctional childhood. She even got me a T-shirt at the trading post with the logo: "The Thing. Mystery of the Past." I'd never been so happy.

We shacked at fleabag motels with names like Apache Tears and the Space Age Lodge. We didn't do anything bad. She kept telling me it was okay, but I knew it wasn't. Instead we just lay on the bed and watched movies. She only liked the ones with happy endings. If a movie looked like it was going to end the wrong way, she'd make me turn off the television and create a different ending. "Movies shouldn't be sad," she said. "Life is already sad enough."

We ate at McDonald's three times a day. I ordered a supersized Big Mac meal every time, while Mother shook her head and scolded me. "Are you trying to kill yourself? That stuff you're eating causes heart disease."

"Those are myths," I said. "Just like the one about cigarettes being bad for you. There's no documented proof. Just hearsay. Besides. It's not like we can afford to eat at the Four Seasons." Then I smiled. "But this frugality isn't going to last forever, Doris. They'll forget about me eventually. Then we can settle down. In New England. In a pretty little Victorian house. On a cobblestone street. No, it won't be long. Before you know it, we'll be in paradise living like kings and queens."

"I hope you're right, Frankie."

"Of course I'm right. Ain't nobody gonna slow us down, Doris, I can guarantee you that much."

But West Texas wasn't that paradise. No, West Texas was an endless sun-baked land of loneliness and desolation with a relentless wind that disheveled the burnt yellow grass and Spanish bayonets. Dust, dirt, derricks, damnation. West Texas was a country all its own, the devil's country, and as soon as we entered its borders, I knew there was no escape for me.

CHAPTER 26

I first noticed the long black Lincoln Continental as we filled up at a ramshackle gas station just outside of Lamesa. Actually that's not quite right. I actually noticed the death mobile as far back as Benson, but it was just a blip in my consciousness, and I hadn't paid any attention to it. But now as the Lincoln slowly edged around the perimeter of the gas station, I became convinced we were being followed. Not wanting to alarm my mother, I made no mention of the car as I ducked inside to pay for the gas and stock up on more Slim Jims and Mountain Dew.

From inside the station I kept close watch on the Lincoln, and when it stopped moving, I tried catching a glimpse of the driver, but the reflection of the sun against the windshield prevented me from seeing anything more than a ghostly silhouette. I paid for the food, gas, and a road map of Texas before heading back outside. As the dust-coated sun shone overhead, I walked slowly to where the Lincoln was parked. The heat rising from the ground made it hard to breathe. I was just a few steps away from the car when the driver hit the accelerator and spun out in reverse. I became blinded momentarily by the dirt and dust. The black car skidded onto the highway, and I watched its taillights get smaller and smaller.

It wasn't until we were a ways up on the crumbling

highway that Mother asked me about the strange car. "Was that the police?" she said.

I shook my head and frowned. "Nah. It was an old friend of mine. Mind handing me a Mountain Dew?"

"Why'd you have to get Mountain Dew?" she said. "You know I hate Mountain Dew."

"That's why I got it. So you wouldn't drink it."

She handed me a soda, but didn't open it for me. I placed it between my legs. "So where do you know him from?" she said.

"Know who?"

"Your friend in the car."

I cracked open the soda and took a long chug. "I met him one night in Hades," I said. "Now open up that Texas road map. We gotta figure out where we're sleeping tonight."

We stopped in a town called Sweetwater, which was anything but. Sweet, I mean. We ate dinner at Buck's Chuck Wagon Barbecue and got a twenty-six-dollar room at the Longhorn Motor Lodge. We watched *Wheel of Fortune*, but I couldn't solve any of the puzzles, even when there were just one or two letters missing.

When the show was over, Mother took off her shirt and disappeared into the bathroom to shower. I flipped through the channels. I came across a nature show about insects. I found out that if you give a scorpion a little liquor, they go crazy and sting themselves to death. I also learned that the female praying mantis bites off the head and upper torso of the male while mating. Despite this humiliation, the male keeps right on copulating. Gotta admire the tenacity.

Mother returned from the bathroom. She wasn't wearing anything but ugliness and unfriendliness. The sight of her uncovered mammary glands got me good and worked up. It was inappropriate, wholly inappropriate. But I kept it together. Mother combed her hair in the mirror, pausing so often to give me a sideways glance.

"What's the matter?" she said in a nasty voice. "Am I making you uncomfortable?"

I shrugged my shoulders. "No," I said. "Just amazed that Hollywood never discovered a beauty like you."

She cackled. "Oh, fuck you, Frankie. You're no prize yourself."

Then she tried getting romantic. She said I owed it to her. She stroked my thigh with her fingers and tugged on my earlobe with her mouth. I pushed her away. "I don't owe you a thing," I said. "You're a goddamn praying mantis." Scowling, I got out of bed and put on my sweat-soaked shirt.

"Wait. Where are you going?"

"Out. Don't wait up."

I grabbed the room key off the dresser, and pushed open the motel door. Outside the air was hot, the moon was dead, and a restless breeze was wandering down the sidewalk.

The business district of Sweetwater, Texas, was small-time. On two of the corners were gas stations: an Exxon and a Sinclair. The prices at the Sinclair were four cents cheaper. I walked past the Tasty Pastry and the Twister Grill until I saw a welcoming Miller neon sign in the darkened windows of a joint called Low Places.

Inside, a couple of baldheaded fellows were sitting at opposite ends of the bar. They both turned their heads simultaneously as I entered. They might have been brothers. I nodded and they both looked back at their beers. I was just a guy. Four or five wooden tables were lined up in the middle of the floor. The bartender, a tall guy with blond hair and a porn-star mustache, appeared and asked if he could get me anything.

"A passport, two tickets to Buenos Aires, and ten thousand dollars in unmarked bills," I said.

"We've just got alcohol," he said unsmilingly.

"Then give me a Miller and some whiskey to wash it down."

The Miller came in a can and the Jim Beam came in a wineglass. I cracked open the beer, opened up my throat, and downed that son-of-a-bitch in three seconds flat. I used my shirt to wipe off my mouth. I was about to get to work on the booze when I noticed that a trashy-looking redhead was sitting in the stool next to mine (they're all trashy-looking, aren't they?). She was wearing a tight red shirt that revealed a blubbery stomach. Her nose was long and crooked, and she had crazy buck teeth. She was staring straight at me.

"You want a drink?" I said.

She nodded her head. "Sure."

"What's your pleasure?"

"I like wine okay."

So I ordered her a glass of the cheapest they had. A 2000 merlot from Oklahoma. She took a couple of sips, smearing the edge of the glass with her purple lipstick. I raised my glass and promptly downed my own poison, eyeing her hungrily all the while.

196

"So what's a pretty girl like you doing in a place like this?" I asked. (I made up that pickup line myself.)

"I'm celebrating."

"Celebrating what?"

"My divorce."

"Good for you."

"My husband was a good man, but he had a disease. He was recently arrested on thirteen counts of child molestation."

"I think I've met him. He was my priest."

She lit a cigarette even though she still had one burning in the ashtray. "I saw you from across the bar," she said.

"I'm hard to miss. What with my good looks and all."

"I've seen you before."

I shook my head. "Probably not. This is my first time in Sweetwater."

"Maybe not here. But somewhere."

"I've got kind of an iconic face," I said.

"What does that mean?"

"It means that I look like a lot of famous people. Johnny Cash, Robert Redford, Sammy Davis Jr.—"

"No, it's none of those people. Give me some time, I'll figure it out. I've got a memory like a hawk."

"Let me buy you another drink."

"Okay. But don't let me get drunk. I'm easy when I'm drunk."

I got her drunk. The bar filled up. The two brothers that were sitting at the counter had left. Loneliness doesn't need company. The redhead babbled on and on about her ex-husband. "It's something the matter with his brain," she said. "Chemical imbalance or something. They're trying medication, but there are no guarantees.

He begged the judge to be castrated, but the judge wouldn't agree to that. Instead he threw him in jail. He'll get eaten alive in there, for sure."

I was getting tired of listening to her. I was feeling restless. I told her that we should go somewhere quieter so we could talk. She shrugged her shoulders. "We could go to the Hotplate Diner," she said. "They've got the best pancakes in town. Well, IHOP is pretty good too."

"I'm not hungry," I said. "Do you live around here?"

"Not too far."

"Let's go there. You live by yourself, right?"

"I've got a dog named Pooch."

"That's all right. I like dogs. I had one as a kid. His name was Duke. I used to throw sticks and he'd chase after them."

"Pooch doesn't do that. He's lazy."

She drove a Hyundai Excel with a Garfield doll suction-cupped to the rear window. The passenger-side door didn't open from the outside, so she had to crawl across the seat and shove it open for me. I climbed inside. I was feeling rebellious so I didn't bother putting on my seat belt. She stuck in a cassette tape and turned up the volume. It was Def Leppard. I didn't much care for Def Leppard, but I didn't complain. She hit the engine and we drove.

The redhead lived in a trailer park called Sol Vista. She parked halfway on the sidewalk and we got out. Inside her home everything smelled like ketchup and cleaning products. I sat down on a stained gray couch while she went into the kitchen to grab us some drinks.

She returned with a couple of beers and sat down on the couch next to me. I cracked mine open and took a sip.

Then I took another sip and it was finished. I crushed it with my hand and set it by my foot. The redhead placed her freckled hand in mine and flashed a buck-toothed grin. "I don't normally do this," she said.

I knew she was lying, but I didn't care. I placed my hand on her thigh. Then I moved it up a few inches. She giggled. "I just wish I could remember where I've seen you."

"It'll come to you," I said. "Mind if we turn off the lights?"

Despite her professed inexperience, she did just fine. She lay on her stomach without complaints. And fortunately for me, I just happened to have a gourd in my pocket. You can never be too prepared. When we were done, her purple lipstick was all smeared and I felt like giving her a right hook to the temple. I resisted.

"That was fun," she said. "I'm going to go take a shower. Wanna join me?"

"Nah, I'm good. I showered last month."

"Okay, honey," she said. "Don't leave me, okay?"

"I wouldn't leave you," I said. "I think I'm in love with you."

She disappeared into the bathroom. Her dog appeared, a miniature poodle. It hopped up on the couch and sniffed my crouch. I shoved him off the couch. He whimpered and moved over by the front door. I turned on the television and finished the redhead's beer. *America's Funniest Home Videos* was on. A man was trying to paint his house, but he fell off the ladder and toppled into a kiddie pool. The live studio audience was hooting with delight.

I changed the channel. The news. A blank-faced bimbo of an anchorwoman was describing my escape from prison.

They flashed my mugshot. I looked like a felon. The anchorwoman spoke in a monotone voice, *"Avicious was set to go on trial for the brutal murder of Marilyn Cook. It is thought that his mother, fifty-seven-year-old Doris Avicious, helped plot the escape. They are believed to be driving a gold 1982 Pontiac Sunbird. Avicious is to be considered armed and very dangerous."*

When they were done talking about me and all the terrible things I'd done, I turned off the television. Then an unpleasant thought started developing in my brain. The redhead kept saying I looked familiar. What if she had seen me on the television? She was bound to figure it out sooner or later, and when she did, she would call the cops. If they learned I had been in Sweetwater, then it would only be a matter of time...

I suddenly became engulfed by a shroud of depression. It was as if my whole world was crumbling around me. All of my best laid plans were imploding, and my courage was transforming to desperation.

In the corner of the room was a guitar. Nothing much, just a cheap little Japanese number. I picked it up and started strumming. And I thought about how I should have listened to my uncle Bob. When I was just a kid, he told me I had one hell of a voice and that I should consider becoming a country singer. That would have been the life. Spending my days traveling from town to town, crooning about heartbreak to thousands of adoring women, getting more ass than a toilet seat. Instead of this. I played a few chords. The guitar was out of tune. The redhead reappeared. She was wearing a white negligee. She smiled that buck-tooth smile. "I didn't know you played the guitar," she said.

"I'm a man of many talents. I also know how to crack open a bottle of beer with my teeth."

"Will you play me a song?"

"Depends. What do you want to hear?"

"I like country. But not the new Nashville stuff. Old-time country."

"That's right," I said. "The authentic stuff." I closed my eyes and started strumming and singing. Something about being so lonesome I could cry.

I stopped suddenly. I looked up at the redhead. Her eyes were filled with tears. "Why'd you stop?" she said. "You've got a beautiful voice."

"The guitar," I said. "It's out of tune. It doesn't sound right."

"It hasn't been played in a while. Not since my ex-husband went away."

I loosened the sixth string. Why had I come here? I could have gone back to the motel. But I didn't. Why the fuck had I come here? Not for love. Sometimes we do things and there is no reason, no motivation. I wasn't born to kill. That was just Marteau, the devil, getting in my head. But why had I come here?

I glanced around the living room. There were no pictures. Nobody would miss her. Nobody would mourn her. I'd come this far. There was no turning back now.

I rose to my feet, gripping the guitar string with both hands. "This one's no good," I said. "Frayed."

"It doesn't matter," she said. "I'll never play it. I don't have any musical talent. When I was a girl, I played the flute, but I had trouble even making a sound. I think it's because of my teeth..."

She prattled on. I stopped listening. I thought about my

mother. Why did I always think about her in times like this? She was waiting at the motel. But she wasn't alone. Of course she wasn't. Marteau was keeping her company. With a rose between his teeth...

I took a step toward the redhead. A sly grin spread across her face. She had no clue. In another minute she'd be dead. So what? We take it all too seriously. We shouldn't. It's all a joke. A big fucking cosmic joke.

"Now I know where I've seen you before," she said in a near whisper.

I gave her a right cross to the jaw. She crumpled to the ground. "But you'll never see me again," I growled. I pounced on top of her. I pulled her back to her knees. Then I wrapped the guitar string around her throat and pulled.

Time passed. I looked down at my hands. They were covered with blood. The redhead wasn't moving much. I thought she might be dead. I released her. She fell to the ground. Her eyes were open and all glazed over. Her white negligee was stained with blood. The guitar string was embedded in her throat.

But she wasn't quite dead yet. She coughed up some blood and spoke. "I know where I've seen you before. You were on my ex-husband's softball team. You played catcher." Then she closed her eyes and died. Pooch sat next to her and licked the blood off her face.

CHAPTER 27

I drove back to the motel. I got out of the car. A bald man with bloodshot eyes and a loosened tie appeared in the glow of the street lamp. I lowered my head and walked past him.

Inside our room, Mother was asleep. I sat down next to her and shook her gently. "Get up," I said. "We've got to go."

Her eyes opened dreamily. "I'm tired," she said.

"Get up," I said again. This time she did. She knew I meant business.

I waited until we were out of Sweetwater before I told my mother what I'd seen on the television. But I didn't tell her about the redhead. There was no point.

"They showed your picture and everything?" she said, a big grin spreading across her face.

"Yeah," I said. "Handsome devil."

"Did they show my picture?"

"No, not that I saw."

"Damn."

"The worst part about it is that they have the make and model of the car. Every cop and sheriff in the western United States is going to be looking for this piece-of-shit Sunbird."

"We should pick up some newspapers," she said. "It's

203

not every day that you become a celebrity. This is your fifteen minutes, Frankie."

"To hell with getting a newspaper, Doris," I said. "We've got to keep moving, and we've got to find us a new car, too."

We headed south on 83, a dark and lonely highway surrounded by endless miles of dirt, mesquite, and shrub oak. Railroad tracks running parallel to the highway glowed in the moonlight. Mom pulled out a piece of bubble gum and started smacking on it, which got me good and annoyed. I turned on the radio. A man was talking about the weather. The temperature was going to be one hundred twelve tomorrow. Hell was getting closer...

We were about halfway between Abilene and Junction when the piece-of-shit Sunbird sank sharply, waking my sleeping mother. "What happened?" she said. I didn't answer. I pulled over to the side of the road, turned off the engine, and stepped outside.

The right-rear tire was as flat as a ten-year-old schoolgirl. I cursed and pounded the side of the car in frustration. I popped open the trunk and searched frantically for a spare. Nothing. I pulled back my greasy blond hair with my hand and spit on the ground. Then I looked out at the endless terrain of death and shook my head. I decided that you just can't win.

I got back into the car and Mother frowned. "Do we have a flat tire?"

I shook my head. "It's a little low, that's all. We should

be able to make it to Junction."

I hit the engine and pulled back onto the highway. We drove for another mile or so until the tire started peeling from the wheel, and the bumper dragged on the pavement. Mother clenched her jaw and shook her head. I turned off the engine and lit a cigarette.

An hour or more passed without the appearance of a single car. Sitting on the hood, I finished off the last of the Slim Jims and Mountain Dew. Mother slept some more in the backseat. The sky was black, and the moon was the color of piss. I tossed my trash in a gully next to the car and opened up the back door. Mother opened her eyes, then closed them again. "We're going to start moving," I said.

"What's the point?"

"Staying stagnant is bad luck. I know that for a fact. We need to start walking to change our karma. And I think you should be the one to flag down any passing automobiles. Male drivers are more likely to stop if they see a pretty damsel in distress."

We walked down the highway in the direction from which we'd already come so that a driver wouldn't see the abandoned Pontiac before he saw us. It was hard to see in the darkness, and I kept tripping over mesquite shrub. Off in the distance a coyote released a blood-curdling howl.

Even though it was nighttime, the air was still heavy and hot. Sweat had soaked through my white T-shirt, and my eyes were beginning to sting from the perspiration that had dribbled into my eyes. I was feeling agitated. Why couldn't things be easy, just one goddamn time?

Mom squeezed my arm tightly and pointed down the highway. I looked up. The ghostly headlights of a car appeared like twin beacons. "All right," I said. "Raise your arms and start waving real frantic-like."

The headlights got closer and closer. When the car was almost upon us, Mother took a step onto the highway and stuck out her thumb. The driver laid on his horn, and gravel and dirt kicked up into our faces. I watched gloomily as the red taillights disappeared into a cloud of dust. Mother cursed and banged her fists against her thighs.

"Take it easy," I said. "There'll be another car coming along soon. Just remember, we're not trying to make it home for Christmas. Our car's broken down. You gotta act desperate. You gotta act real desperate."

We continued walking. We were now a mile or more away from our car, and I was beginning to feel fatigued. I decided it would be a good time to conserve energy, considering we didn't have any water.

"There's a nice big rock just up ahead," I said. "We can rest there until the next car arrives. But we've got to stay alert. She'll be coming around the mountain when she comes."

We sat down and Mom rested her head on my shoulder. I placed my arm around her and pulled her close. I closed my eyes and took a deep breath. It had been a long day. Longer than a boa constrictor tied together with a...with a...ah to hell with it.

It wasn't until the sky had become pale and the stars had faded away, that another car finally appeared. Mother got up from the rock and stood in the middle of the highway, waving her arms like windshield wipers. For a few moments the car continued speeding, and I thought Mother would be road kill, but then it slowed and finally came to a stop about ten yards in front of where she stood.

The young man who stepped out of the black Honda Civic wasn't angry, or at least he didn't appear to be angry. "Are you stranded, ma'am?" he asked.

"Our car broke down," she said. "Flat tire. We don't have a spare."

"We could sure use a lift," I said, stepping onto the asphalt, my sudden appearance startling him.

He was tall and gangly with a sharp slanted nose and blue eyes that seemed too close together. He was trying to grow a goatee, but it was wispy and patchy. He was wearing a University of Texas T-shirt, his long arms dangling at his side.

The young man furrowed his brow and looked contemplative for several moments. Then, after rationalizing the situation in his head, he made up his mind. And he did what any good-natured liberal college student would do. "Hop in," he said. "I'll give you a ride to the next town."

I crawled into the backseat, allowing Mommy to have shotgun. Clothes and CDs were piled on the seat. He apologized. "No worries," I said. "We sure do appreciate the lift. We don't have any water, and we were starting to worry about that mean ol' sun rising."

He got the car into gear and pulled back on the highway. Some crappy classic rock was blasting, and he quickly turned it down. Then he pumped up the air-conditioning and nodded, trying to think of something clever to say.

"So where are you all heading?" was all he could come up with.

"New England," I said quickly.

"No shit?" he said. "I'm from New Hampshire originally."

"Oh yeah?"

"Yeah. I got out of there as quickly as I could. The winters suck. Cold and gray. And the summers are too muggy."

"Well, we're not going to New Hampshire," I said.

"That's good. Where are you going then?"

"Probably Pennsylvania."

"That's not New England."

My jaw tightened. "Close enough."

I looked out the window. We were nearing where the Sunbird was parked. I pulled my pistol out of the front of my jeans and made sure it was loaded. Neither Mother nor the young man noticed.

"What's your name?" Mother asked.

"Jason."

"You seem like a nice boy."

"Thank you."

As soon as I saw our piece-of-shit car, I stuck the pistol in the back of Jason's head and told him to pull over. Instinctively, he turned and looked back. When he saw the pistol, he let out a little feminine shriek. "I'm not gonna hurt you," I said. "We just need your car is all."

"What are you doing, Frank?" Mother said.

"Don't worry about it," I said. "Pull over, pal."

He stopped about a hundred yards past the Sunbird. I ordered him to stick it in reverse, and he did. When we were directly next to our car, I told him to get out. At first he didn't make a move. I cocked the pistol, and that seemed to jump-start him. He opened the door and stepped outside, a constipated look on his face.

"Don't hurt him," Mother said.

"You just wait here."

I pushed the driver's seat forward and pulled myself outside. I stuck the pistol in the small of his back and handed him my car keys. "Open the trunk," I said.

He tried unlocking the trunk, but his hands were just shaking too much. I shouted at him, but that didn't help. Finally, I grabbed the keys and opened it up myself. "Now get inside."

He looked at me plaintively and shook his head. "Please, mister," he said, his voice suddenly steady. "Don't make me do that. I'll die in there."

"I'm sorry," I said. "I just can't take any chances. My karma's been bad, real bad, and I can't leave it up to the Devil-God anymore."

He continued standing there, his face ashen. "The sun's beginning to rise. It's supposed to be a hundred and twelve today. I'll never survive."

I lowered my weapon. "I don't want you to die. You seem like a nice kid. I'll tell you what I'll do. I'll call the cops in an hour or so, tell them where you are. By that time I'll be long gone, and you'll still be alive."

"Well—"

"The way I figure things, you don't have much of a choice," I said, jabbing the gun into his ribs.

Eventually, he crawled into the trunk. It was a tight squeeze, but things could have been worse for him. Of course, I never had plans of calling the cops, that would have been far too risky, but the thought of him burning to death in that trunk was too much for me. I had nothing against Jason from New Hampshire and had no reason to make him suffer. Instead, I raised the gun and fired four times until I was pretty sure he was dead. Then I slammed the trunk shut.

As you can probably imagine, my mother was none too thrilled that I had killed her friend Jason. "What'd you have to do that for?" she said when I got back into the car. "He didn't do anything to you."

I touched her shoulder and pursed my lips. "I did it out of mercy," I said.

"Mercy? That didn't look like mercy to me."

"Listen. I've got to make some tough decisions if we're gonna survive this little adventure we've embarked on. If you'd rather be in charge, just let me know. I don't relish the role, believe me."

Mother was plenty upset, but there was nothing I could do about it. I stuck the car into gear and pulled onto the highway. Since I wasn't used to driving a stick, I stalled a couple of times before getting the hang of it. Mother kept jerking in an exaggerated manner every time I shifted gears. There was no doubt she needed a major attitude adjustment. Once I figured out the stick thing, the Civic rode much better than the Sunbird. I figured I'd made the right move by killing that boy. About time I'd done something right.

The sun was beginning to rise. I turned on the radio and found an Abilene country station, but it was full of static. I think Patsy Cline was singing, but it might have been Loretta Lynn. I turned it off. Mother closed her eyes.

Oil wells dotted the landscape, and the heat rose from the blistering pavement. I turned on the air-conditioning full blast, but it was a losing battle. It was going to be hot today. It was going to be mighty hot today.

As I drove, I realized just how tired I was. Exhaustion was seeping through my bones. My eyelids were heavy, and I kept shaking my head, trying to regain my focus. I glanced over at Mother. Her mouth was open, and she was snoring gently.

I lit a cigarette and inhaled deeply, the smoke filling up my brain. I opened the window. A wave of searing air entered the car. I glanced at myself in the rearview mirror and felt sick to my stomach. I stepped on the gas, trying to make things feel right, but you can never escape from yourself, can you, and that's a crying shame.

An hour passed before Mother woke up. She stretched her body and looked at me like I were a stranger. I nodded at her and kept my eyes focused on those hypnotic yellow lines. "Where are we?" she said.

"Just outside of Uvalde."

"How long do you think it'll take until they find us?"

"What the hell are you talking about?"

"They're gonna find my old car. Then they're gonna look in the trunk. It won't take long for them to figure out what car we're driving now."

"We'll cross that bridge when we come to it."

"We're gonna die, aren't we, Frankie?"

I gave her a sideways glance. "Don't worry about it," I said. "Like you said. Dying's the easy part."

She rested her head against the window and sighed. "It's just that I can't stop thinking about him."

"Who?"

"That young boy. Jason."

"Come on now."

"I wonder what his parents were like or if he had a girlfriend. I'll bet he did. He seemed nice."

I grinned and gripped the steering wheel tighter.

"I just don't understand why you've got to go killing innocent people, people who've done you no wrong."

"You're naïve," I growled. "There's no such thing as an innocent person. Never has been, never will be. We're all guilty in the eyes of the nonexistent Lord because his standards are so goddamn high. Morality's not something everyone can afford, but he just doesn't understand that. He acts like we're all on a level playing field. Well, we're not. I was born in the center of hell, and I've been digging like a madman ever since in hopes of escaping. Except instead of a shovel, all he gave me was a cracked teaspoon."

CHAPTER 28

We were less than fifty miles from the Mexico border when our honeymoon ended. Vaguely aware of muted sirens, I glanced in my rearview mirror and saw the flashing of police lights. Dread spread through my veins. Mother sat up straight and glanced over her shoulder. Then she shook her head. "You better pull over," she said.

"Like hell," I said. I leaned forward in my seat and stepped on the accelerator. Pretty soon I had the Honda up to a hundred, then over a hundred. But the cop car kept pace with me. Mother started shouting at me. "You're gonna get us killed! Pull over!" She tried grabbing a hold of the steering wheel, but I shoved her away. They weren't going to catch me alive. They weren't going to send me back to that cage. I wasn't an animal.

We might have made it too, but they'd set up a roadblock. At first I couldn't believe my eyes; I didn't think I was important enough for them to go through all that trouble. But as we got closer and closer, it became obvious there was no escaping this time. I wiped the sweat from my brow. "Goddamn those motherfuckers," I shouted. "Can't they just live and let live?" Then, "Open up the glove compartment and hand me that gun."

"No, Frankie. I won't do it."

"Now don't you start with me," I said. "I need that gun, and I need it now."

"Go to hell."

I hit her in the cheek with the back of my hand. Her head bounced off the window and she groaned. I reached across her body and pulled open the glove compartment. I grabbed the pistol. Mother tried stopping me by yanking on my arm and biting my wrist. I shouted in pain but managed to keep control of the weapon. The car swerved, and it took great effort to prevent it from ducktailing. The roadblock was now less than a quarter of a mile away. I could see a couple of police officers standing outside their cars, waving for me to slow down. I raised the gun to the windshield and started firing. The shots were deafening, and the glass shattered. Hot desert air raced through the broken windshield, taking my breath away. Up ahead, I saw the officers duck behind their cars and raise their rifles. There was a narrow corridor between the two police cars, and I knew that was our only hope.

As we sped through the two parked cars, I heard gunshots coming from every direction, smashing into the metal and glass. Everything exploded. For a moment, I thought I was dead. Smoke and dust and glass and blood were everywhere. The Honda continued barreling down the highway for a while until I heard a loud thud. Then everything was quiet.

When I came to, I slapped my face a few times, rubbed my eyes with the backs of my hands, and stared at the mess sitting next to me in the passenger seat. Her front teeth had been knocked out, and her nose had been shoved out of place. Blood was seeping from a gaping hole in the side of her head. Her eyes were still open. I closed her eyelids with my thumbs. I felt like I was going to be sick.

I tried opening the driver's-side door, but it was jammed. Cursing, I crawled over my mother's body and kicked open the door. I tumbled out of the car—which was stuck in a dry arroyo—and struggled to my feet. I reached back inside and grabbed my gun from beneath Mother's feet. A half mile back, I could see five or more police cars edging cautiously through the dust, their sirens echoing across the bleak wasteland.

I ran across the desert floor. The only sounds I could hear were the brush and cacti crunching beneath my feet, and the heavy gasps escaping from my mouth. I didn't look back. I darted through the mesquite black brush waiting for a bullet to tear through my spine.

I must have run for an hour or more without stopping. I tied my T-shirt around my head, trying to protect myself from the sun that was becoming meaner and more resolute. The skin on my chest was burning.

I knew the police were still in pursuit and they would soon be sending dogs and helicopters to track me down, but I couldn't go another step. I found some remnants of shade beneath a gnarled mesquite tree. I sat down and laid my pistol on the dirt next to me. Unless I found water soon I would die out here in the desert all alone, and eventually the buzzards would have a feast on good ol' Frankie Avicious. Nobody could survive for long out here in this heat. It was a shame things had to end this way. I'd never been given a break, not a single break, and now I was going to die in the most torturous manner possible. The Devil-God was having a good laugh somewhere.

I closed my eyes but didn't sleep. I thought about my mother and felt sad and angry all at once. She was the only person I'd ever loved. It wasn't right. She didn't have to die.

I rested for a half an hour or maybe more. Then I pulled myself to my feet and started moving again. Without any replenishment, I had stopped sweating. My body temperature was rising to match the air around it, and sharp pains were shooting through my muscles. I spit on the ground and watched the saliva sizzle.

Hope returned momentarily when the clouds began billowing overhead and the wind started blowing. If it would only rain—just for a short while—then maybe I could survive for a few more hours. But lady luck was nothing more than a prick tease. The rain fell from the clouds in a steady sheet of mist, but evaporated long before it reached the ground. Soon the sun reappeared in all its uncontained rage.

I trudged on. Blisters were developing on my shoulders. I removed the shirt from my head and pulled it back over my torso. A rattlesnake slithered past my feet and a helicopter appeared out of nowhere, circling like a buzzard. Death had me surrounded.

I needed water. Goddamn it, I needed water. I remembered hearing that cactuses sometimes had water inside them. I stood in front of a towering saguaro and started kicking it with my boot. I couldn't even dent the motherfucker. I cocked my pistol and fired a couple of times, the shots echoing throughout the sizzling air. I was hoping water would start streaming like piss, but there was no such luck. I heard the faint drone of the helicopter, still circling. Locating the bullet hole in the saguaro, I cocked my arm back and punched, hoping to open up a bigger hole. A sharp pain shot through my wrist, and I cursed. The saguaro wagged its finger at me and shook its head. "Don't you be stealing any life from me, boy," it said.

What about underground? Wasn't there sometimes water buried beneath the dirt? Yes there was! With a grin on my face, I got down on my knees and started digging maniacally with my hands. Dig, Frankie Avicious, dig!

With newfound energy, I settled into my project. Unfortunately, the red dirt was sun baked, and the going was extremely tedious. I was feeling lightheaded, but I pressed on. The hours passed, but the blazing sun seemed to remain frozen in the middle of the sky. My digging became slower and more laborious until eventually I couldn't go on. I sat down on my ass and pulled my legs toward me. Then I rolled into the fetal position and closed my eyes. I was going to die, and I didn't give a damn. Fuck this life. Fuck this world.

CHAPTER 29

When he appeared before me, I wasn't surprised. I guess you could say I was expecting him. I opened my eyes and blinked a few times, then feebly raised my hand to shield my eyes from the sun. At first I could only see his silhouette, but as my eyes adjusted to the light, he began to take form. He was wearing a serape and carrying his briefcase. A thin grin was spread across his gaunt face, and his pale skin seemed almost translucent. And then there were his eyes, or rather lack thereof. Beneath his eyelids there was nothing but black voids.

He rested his briefcase on the ground and knelt down beside me. "It's good to see you, Frankie, although I must say, you don't look well."

I mustered a grin, then attempted to spit at him. The saliva dribbled weakly down my chin. My lips and skin and tongue were cracked, and blood was trickling from my nostrils. The sun splintered into fragments across the desert floor.

Marteau placed his skeletal hand on my forehead and smoothed back my hair. I tried moving away, but I no longer had any control over my body. "There, there," he whispered. "Everything's going to be okay." An involuntary shriek escaped from my mouth. Moments later, in one powerful spasm, I vomited the remainder of my life onto my chest and shoulders. Marteau giggled before removing his serape and using it to wipe off the mess.

"You're dehydrated, of course," he said. "That's the crux of your problem. You're lucky I found you out here, Frankie. Dying of thirst is an agonizing way to go."

Marteau opened his briefcase and pulled out a long, warped water bottle and a pair of badly chipped wineglasses. Unhurriedly, he filled up both glasses. He placed one on the ground next to me, but I was unable to move my arms. Shaking his head with feigned concern, he used one of his hands to prop up my head. He lifted the glass to my mouth and tipped it slowly forward. Greedily, I swallowed down the water, pausing momentarily while he refilled the glass.

When I had drunk a half gallon or more, I was finally able to pull myself up. I leaned against the mesquite tree and wiped the blood from my nose with the back of my hand. Life gradually returned to my veins, and Marteau regarded me with bemusement.

"You're alone," he finally said. "What happened to your mother?"

"She's dead."

"A shame. Such a classy woman. And she played her role perfectly."

"Role?"

"She was only following orders, Frankie. As am I."

"What the hell are you talking about? Orders from whom?"

"That doesn't matter, Frankie, really it doesn't."

The skin on my face was itching. "You don't fool me," I said, "and you don't scare me."

"I'm glad because those were never my intentions."

"What the fuck were your intentions?"

"I was sent to guide you, Frankie, to help you find your destiny."

I laughed. "You did a hell of a job, Jack."

A vulture skulked overhead. The heat pressed down on me, a blanket of fire. Marteau rose to his feet and nodded. "It's time to go, Frankie," he said.

"Time to go where?"

"You know where."

A sudden panic ran through my body, a panic so intense that I lost my breath for several moments and found myself gasping for air. When I recovered, Marteau had his back turned toward me and was walking slowly across the chaparral-covered floor. He didn't look back. His figure became smaller and smaller.

I got to my feet. I picked up the pistol and followed after him. Despite walking quickly, I didn't seem to be making up any ground, his shadowy outline remaining a dream far in the distance.

I alternated between running and walking for what might have been an hour. I kept scratching at my face, and large chunks of skin were flaking into my hand. I clenched my jaw and stuck my hands in my pocket, resolute not to touch my flaming skin. The sun had reached its peak in the sky, and everything was absolutely still.

I stepped over rattlers and lizards and cacti and shrubs, all the while keeping a close watch on my adversary. At some point I noticed he'd stopped moving, or perhaps he was walking backward. I gripped the pistol tighter. The respite of life that had been granted to me was beginning to wear off, and I felt the familiar dizziness and nausea returning. My legs felt like overcooked spaghetti, and it took every last ounce of will to continue moving.

I finally caught up to him. He was leaning against a dead sycamore tree, adjusting his forever-broken watch. When he saw me, he nodded and started whistling a vaguely familiar tune. He winked. "We're almost there."

I shook my head. "I can't go on."

"It's just up ahead, past the arroyo. Can't you see it?"

I glanced past his shoulder. I saw nothing but forever desolation. I had had enough. I dropped my pistol on the ground and gave it a boot for good measure. Then I sat on a rock and started to cry. I cried like I'd never cried before. I don't know where all the tears came from. I cried like a teenage prom queen runner-up cutting red onions after burying her dog in the backyard. I cried like a teething unfed baby with diaper rash and a bad case of diarrhea. My chest and jeans quickly became soaked with saltwater. Marteau placed his hand on my shoulder. "You're frustrated," he said. "But there's no use in fighting anymore. You did what you did, and now you need to pay the price. Be thankful though, Frankie. At least you had yourself some fun while it lasted."

I looked up and scowled. "There's no fun in living."

He shrugged his shoulders. "We're almost there, Frankie. But we've got to keep moving."

The factory appeared like a dream, obscured in the sun-drenched dust and dirt that swirled across the desert. I took a few steps forward and stopped. The salesman placed his hand on my shoulder and smiled. "Welcome home, Frankie."

Everything about the building was identical, from the windowless redbrick veneer, to the newly polished "Sunshine Foods" sign out front. Black steam billowed from smokestacks, and the factory whistle moaned. The only difference was the setting, out here in the middle of the inhospitable desert, endless miles from civilization. I turned toward the salesman and shook my head. "This isn't real. None of this is real."

He smiled grimly. "I'm afraid it is, Frankie. This is all that's left."

Terror spread through my body. For the first time I understood. I grabbed a hold of Marteau's wrist. "I didn't have a choice," I pleaded. "I was born bad."

"I know, Frankie, I know."

"Isn't there something we can do? Isn't there somebody who can stop this from happening?"

"Close your eyes," he said. "It makes it easier."

CHAPTER 30

The next thing I remember was hearing screams. Not your typical roller-coaster screams, but ancient blood-curdling shrieks full of terror and dread. And beneath the shrieks, I heard the whining of power saws and the muffled *pop, pop, pop* from the captive bolt gun. I placed my hands over my ears, trying in vain to mute the terrible sounds. Then I caught my first whiff of the sickening odor of newly slaughtered flesh, and the quiet reeking of carcasses hanging in the freezer storage area.

I opened my eyes. I found myself alone, standing in a metal barred chute, no larger than a prison cell. On the ground were blood and vomit and shit and flesh. I panicked. I started flailing and thrashing around, trying to break free of my restraints, to no avail. My own screams mixed with the others, creating a chorus of terror. I called out for Marteau, but he was nowhere to be found. Fear was nibbling at my insides, gnawing on my intestines.

Minutes passed, agonizingly slow. Finally, the dense steel door rose. The smells and sounds intensified. When the door was completely open, I was greeted with a sight so horrifying that my body started convulsing uncontrollably. In front of me were the usual going-ons of a slaughterhouse—the shooting and cutting and stabbing and slicing—except instead of cattle being shackled and disassembled, there were human beings. Terrified men and women were being chained by their feet and lifted to various stations where they were systematically butchered.

I could not see the faces of the workers because they all wore white surgical masks. Three of them appeared in my chute, wordlessly. One of them was holding a large device I recognized to be a captive bolt gun. I looked around, searching for a way to escape, but there was none. The men walked slowly toward me. My body was weak. I tried fighting them off, but it was no use. Two of them grabbed a hold of my arms and held me steady, while the man with the stun gun pressed it against my forehead. I screamed in agony as the nail entered through my skull. The men released their hold. I collapsed to the ground, paralyzed. My eyes remained open, and I was able to perceive what was happening around me but was incapable of resisting, incapable of moving at all.

I heard the rattle of the shackles. One of the men—they all seemed identical to me—grabbed a hold of my leg and fastened the chain around it. Moments later, I was hoisted into a hanging position. The trolley swing moved slowly across the killing floor. Another man appeared, a blood-stained knife dangling at his side. I looked into his empty eyes and knew right away who it was. I tried saying something, but my mouth wouldn't work. The screams around me had ceased, and all was quiet. Wrinkles appeared around his eyes indicating a smile, and he pressed the knife to my throat. I felt the coldness of the blade cutting through my flesh, then the warmth of blood draining from my body. My eyes rolled into the back of my head. Cruel laughter filled my brain.

I traveled along the rail for several minutes, then jerked

to a stop. I became vaguely aware of a low humming sound. The humming became louder. Out of the corner of my eye I saw another masked worker approaching me, carrying an electric knife. I tried screaming but there was no noise.

He started at my toes and worked slowly, peeling the skin from my legs and my chest and my ass and my back and my arms and my neck. My face was torn off, my eyes, tongue, and ears removed. For a moment I carried the pain and agony of every man who'd ever died. Oh, Jesus, oh Jesus, don't forsake me.

I knew what was coming next. I watched from above. A ghost with a chain saw. First my legs. Then my arms. Then my head. Then there was nothing except for my soul. And it was burning.

Jon Bassoff was born in 1974 in New York City and currently lives with his family in a ghost town somewhere in Colorado. His mountain gothic novel, *Corrosion*, has been translated in French and German and was nominated for the *Grand Prix de Litterature Policiere*, France's biggest crime fiction award. Three of his novels, *Corrosion*, *The Incurables*, and *The Disassembled Man* have been adapted for the big screen. For his day job, Bassoff teaches high school English where he is known by students and faculty alike as the deranged writer guy. He is a connoisseur of tequila, hot sauces, psychobilly music, and flea-bag motels.

BOOKS

On the following pages are a few
more great titles from the
Down & Out Books publishing family.

For a complete list of books and to
sign up for our newsletter,
go to DownAndOutBooks.com.

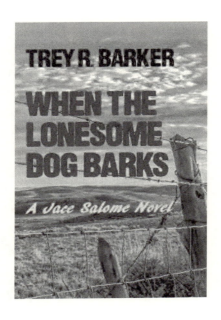

When the Lonesome Dog Barks
A Jace Salome Novel
Trey R. Barker

Down & Out Books
November 2017
978-1-946502-14-8

After discovering a fight club amongst the inmates in her jail, Zachary County Deputy Sheriff Jace Salome soon realizes the darkest recesses of her imagination cannot keep up with reality. Inexplicably, the fights seem to be directed from someone outside the jail. This is a world of technology and online predators, and the stakes are much higher than her pay-grade.

Worse still…Jace Salome has to face this case alone.

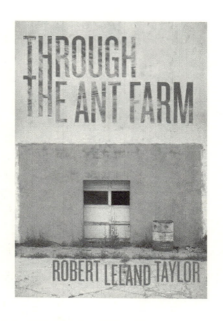

Through the Ant Farm
Robert Leland Taylor

ABC Group Documentation,
an imprint of Down & Out Books
July 2017
978-1-943402-94-6

I'm not really retarded, as far as I know, but I suppose some of the other inmates around here might think so. Not because I killed my daddy, but because of the social thing—I'm just not very good at it…

And it's a shame, too, because I know God would've been very proud of me, saving his little creatures and all. There's not a doubt in my mind.

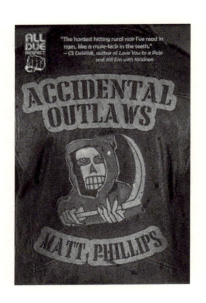

Accidental Outlaws
Matt Phillips

All Due Respect,
an imprint of Down & Out Books
December 2017
978-1-946502-44-5

Three linked crime novellas that follow working class anti-heroes as they indulge in theft, murder, and lawless shenanigans. Ain't no cops running things out this way. In "Mesa Boys," Ronnie plots a haphazard heist with a twisted con man. In "The Feud," tough-as-nails Rex lets his resentment for a local pot dealer cloud his judgement. And, in "Bar Burning," a mysterious drifter goes toe-to-toe with his new lady's psychotic ex-husband.

Dead Clown Blues
A Carnegie Fitch Mystery Fiasco
R. Daniel Lester

Shotgun Honey
an imprint of Down & Out Books
September 2017
978-1-946502-02-5

Carnegie Fitch, once-upon-a-time drifter and now half-assed private eye, has a sharp tongue, a cheap suit and dog-bite marks on his fedora. Yes, that's just how he rolls through the downtown streets of Vancouver, BC, aka Terminal City, circa 1957, a land of neon signs, 24-hour diners and slumming socialites. And on the case of a lifetime, a case of the dead clown blues.

Made in the USA
Middletown, DE
17 June 2019